THE MARK OF THE ANGEL

THE MARK OF THE ANGEL

NANCY HUSTON

MCARTHUR & COMPANY
TORONTO

First published in French in 1998 as *L'Empreinte de l'ange*
by Actes Sud Publishers, France and Leméac Publishers, Québec.

English version by the author.

This Canadian edition published by
McArthur & Company
322 King Street West, Suite 402
Toronto, Ontario M5V 1J2

Canadian Cataloguing in Publication Data

Huston, Nancy, 1953–
The mark of the angel

ISBN 1-55278-084-8

I. Title.

PS8565.U8255M37 1999   C813'.54   C99-931672-9
PR9199.3.H87M37 1999

My thanks to the Canada Council for the Arts, who
awarded me a generous grant to write this book before it was
even a project; and to Cynthia Liebow, for the meticulousness
with which she helped me revise the English version.

Manufactured in the United States of America

FIRST EDITION

For Séverine A.

How can we compare sufferings?
Each person's suffering is the most important.
But what enables us to go on?
Only sound, which comes and goes
like water amongst the stones.

GÖRAN TUNSTRÖM

Now, now,
as music always says,
don't cry.

INGEBORG BACHMANN

Our story begins in the month of May 1957, in the city of Paris.

France is sizzling with nervous energy. In the twelve years since the end of the war, the country has gone through twenty-four governments and eighty-nine proposed amendments to the constitution. But people don't seem too concerned — according to a recent survey, only 41 percent of French conversations revolve around politics. Subject number one, with a score of 47 percent, is Brigitte Bardot (she's decided not to go to Cannes this year, and the *Figaro* has expressed its indignation).

All in all, life is great. Modern. Unemployment doesn't exist, cars are chrome-fitted, living rooms glow with the gray light of TV, film directors are making new waves, babies are booming and Picasso is just commencing his Fall of Icarus, a giant wall painting for UNESCO — which, he promises, will depict "peaceful humanity turning its gaze toward the happy future."

Naturally, not everything is perfect. Here and there, even in France, there are signs that humanity still has a little progress to make.

For instance, four hundred thousand young Frenchmen, who have completed their basic training in Germany, are currently in Algeria for the purpose of — oh, not a war or anything like that, simply, well, a kind of pacification process that is becoming a little sticky.

Or for instance . . .

Oh, be my Dante and I'll be your Virgil! Give me your hand, give me your hand. Have no fear, I won't abandon you, I promise, I'll remain always by your side as we go spiraling slowly down the stairs. . . .

I
—

There she is.

Saffie.

Standing there.

Her face very pale. Or to be more accurate — pallid.

She's standing at a door in a shadowy hallway on the third floor of a handsome old house on the Rue de Seine, about to knock. She knocks. Her gestures are vague, preoccupied.

She just arrived in Paris a few days ago — a Paris trembling through raindrops on filthy windows — a gray, foreign, leaden, dripping Paris. The Gare du Nord. Having gotten on the train at Düsseldorf.

Twenty years old.

Neither well nor badly dressed. Gray pleated skirt, white long-sleeved blouse, white ankle socks, black leather purse, matching shoes — rather ordinary clothing — but when you look at her closely, Saffie herself is anything but ordinary. She's strange. Not easy, at first glance, to put your finger on what's strange about her. And then — ah — you see it: it's her utter lack of hurry.

In the apartment, on the other side of the door she's just knocked on, someone is practicing Marin Marais's *Folies d'Espagne* on the flute. The flutist goes over the same phrase six or seven times, trying to smooth it out, preserve the rhythm, keep from hitting any wrong notes — and finally manages to play it to perfection. But Saffie isn't listening. She's doing absolutely nothing other than standing at the door. Nearly five minutes have elapsed since she knocked on it, and no one's come to open it. She hasn't knocked a second time, nor has she turned to leave.

The concierge, who saw her entering the building earlier and has just gotten to the third floor to distribute the mail (she takes the elevator up to the top of the building then walks down floor by floor) is taken aback to see the young stranger standing motionless in front of Monsieur Lepage's door.

"What! . . ." she exclaims.

She's an obese and ugly woman; her face is dotted with hairy moles; but her eyes are filled with treasures of kindness and wisdom where her fellow human beings are concerned.

"But — he's at home, Monsieur Lepage! Did you ring the bell?"

Saffie understands French. She speaks it, too, albeit imperfectly.

"No," she says. "I knocked."

Her voice is soft, deep, husky — a Marlene Dietrich sort of voice, minus the mannerisms. Her accent is by no means grotesque.

"But he can't hear you!" says Mademoiselle Blanche. "You must ring!"

She leans insistently on the bell and the music breaks off. Triumphant smile from Mademoiselle Blanche.

"There you go!"

Bending forward with difficulty, she slips Monsieur Lepage's mail under his door and disappears into the stairwell.

Saffie still hasn't moved. Her immobility is quite astounding.

The door is flung open. Light floods the shadowy hallway.

"What the hell! . . ."

Raphael Lepage isn't really angry, he's just pretending. It seems to him a bit inappropriate to ring so aggressively when one's looking for a job. Saffie's silence, however, strikes him with the force of a blow. Calms him down. Shuts him up.

And now, this man and this woman who've never met stand on either side of the threshold, staring at each other. Or rather, he stares at her and she . . . just stands there. Raphael is nonplussed. He's never seen anything like it in his life. A woman who can be standing right in front of you, yet somehow not be there.

.   .   .   .   .   .

When the doorbell's strident F-natural sounded a moment earlier, he'd been in the middle of playing a high F-sharp. He'd broken off, nerves jangling with the dissonance. Distracted. Suspended between the two worlds. Neither here, where the air rippled and streamed with sonorous shades, nor there, where young women answered his advertisement in the *Figaro*.

"Damn!" Carefully setting his Louis Lot on the blue velvet of its open case, he'd walked across the living-room rugs and down the hardwood floor of the hallway. Everything in the apartment around him was refined and burnished and genteel; wall tapestries and smooth oak furnishings glistened and gleamed, whispering affluence and good taste; reds and browns and golds reigned and the textures cried out to be caressed. A million motes of dust, however, danced in the shafts of sunlight — the whole thing *did* need to be kept up.

His mother had given him careful instructions on this subject the previous week before she packed up — lock, stock, barrel, and maid — to leave for their house in Burgundy, handing over the Paris apartment to him. First, she'd told him, he'd have to compose a proper ad for the *Figaro,* and second, handpick the prospective employees. "Watch out for the quick-fingered ones!" she'd warned him. "They're easy to spot; their eyes move in zigzags."

"Seek maid for light housework. Room and board. Culinary skills required."

A text reduced to the bare essentials, chosen by Raphael because he hated playing the role of the bourgeois, and by Saffie because it didn't contain the phrases "references required" or "good morality."

When she'd called an hour ago, Raphael had noticed she had an accent. He couldn't have said from what country, but her French seemed a bit shaky. This was actually an asset, as far as he was concerned. The last thing he wanted was a chatterbox like Maria-Felice, the Portuguese maid who'd been his mother's confidante for as long as he could remember. He intended to explain to his future employee that he was ultrasensitive to sound. That it would be out of the question for her to do the vacuuming when he was at home. That she mustn't dream of humming while she dusted the furniture. That dropping a pot or pan in the kitchen during his practice hours would be cause for dismissal.

Now he yanks the door open, feigning anger —

"What the hell! . . ."

Blinks, as his eyes adjust to the darkness in the hallway. Tries to check out her expression for shiftiness, and is brought up short.

Because.

A smile that looks painted on. Arms hanging loosely at her sides. A slender body. This is all he has time to notice before he falls headlong into the well of her eyes. Green and opaque, like two fragments of jade. Placid pools, unshimmering, unmoving.

Yes — from the beginning, it is Saffie's indifference that fascinates Raphael. Captivates him. Bewitches him. From the beginning, even before he learns her name, he can see that this young woman doesn't give a damn whether she gets the job or not. Whether she's alive or dead. She seems to have been somehow thrown out into the world, dispassionate and unfearing. She displays neither the hypocritical, calculating modesty of well-brought-up girls nor the equally calculating impudence of whores. She's just there. He's never seen anything like it.

"Please come in," he says at last, in a totally different voice, gentle and filled with respect.

As Saffie crosses the threshold, he sees that her movements are just as motionless and indifferent as her eyes. His stomach leaps wildly when he closes the door behind her, and he has to stop to catch his breath, his eyes riveted to the wooden doorjamb, before he can turn around.

He then precedes her down the hallway, feeling her empty green gaze on the back of his head.

In the living room, he sits down on the couch and motions for her to take a seat in the armchair across from him. She obeys, wordlessly. Seeing her eyes glued to the rug, he rapidly surveys her appearance. Longish hair held back in a ponytail by a plain rubber band. High forehead, prominent cheekbones, lipstick-coated lips, ears like perfect seashells studded with false pearl earrings, finely sculpted nose and carefully arched eyebrows — a well-modeled face, on which it's impossible to read anything. There's no shyness in it, no simpering, nothing. The makeup and jewelry clash with the spectacular neutrality of her features. Raphael stares at her in a daze.

Stupidly, he reaches out a hand and grabs the little bronze bell to summon the maid, ask her to bring them some coffee — then shakes his head, laughing inwardly: there is no maid, she's the maid, where are we, who are you, my dear . . .

"You are Mademoiselle? . . ."

"My name is Zaffie," she says — and, when he asks her to repeat it, then to spell it, it turns out that it begins with an *S;* her name is Saffie but she pronounces it "Zaffie," because she's German.

German. The word itself virtually taboo in this apartment on the Rue de Seine. His mother called them neither Krauts nor Boches nor Jerries nor even Germans, she simply said *they,* in fact more often than not she didn't say anything at all, merely pressed her lips together until all you could see was a red horizontal line in the middle of her narrow bony face — because, even if her husband hadn't exactly died fighting them, it was still the Germans' fault that Madame Trala-Lepage had found herself widowed at the age of forty, with so many years left to live and practically no hope of finding another man to love her, cherish her, shower her with gifts. Raphael's father, a professor of history at the Sorbonne whose specialty had been the secular and humanist tradition in France, had met his end in the quarter of Les Halles in the fateful month of January 1942, when a pack of frenzied housewives had hurled themselves upon a truck of potatoes, overturning it with him underneath. (What the great professor had been doing in the Rue Quincampoix at six in the morning *before* perishing under the truck is another question. . . .)

Two years later, the Occupation army had massacred four Resistance fighters right in front of their house and Raphael, his hands gripping the wrought-iron railing of the balcony, had leaned out the living-room window to see the pool of blood — the shots had ceased a full minute earlier, it was all over, the young men were no longer young men but corpses, a heap of inert flesh, and how not to stare at that?, so Raphael had stuck out his lovely head covered with soft black curls as far as possible, craning his neck, widening his gentle brown eyes to see — not death, but the truth behind death, behind the messy mass of arms and legs, the bloody embrace of four comrades fallen together — and then — Hortense's hysterical scream piercing the eardrum of her musical offspring — "*What are you doing?* Have you gone berserk? Shut the window, for God's sake! You're all I have left in the world, I don't want them to take everything from me! . . ."

Raphael is certain that, had it not been for his mother's explicit and unshakable opposition, he would have joined the Resistance movement at the end of '43 (he could have then, he was fifteen and longed to be part of the romantic ranks of the Forces Françaises de l'Intérieur), but, his father being dead and his mother having no one left but him, he'd had to support the struggle against the Germans in purely moral and spiritual ways. It was for the same reason, namely the semi-glorious death of his father while fighting (in the broad sense of the term) for his country, that Raphael hadn't been called up to serve in Algeria. Instead, he'd gone on to the Conservatory. And done brilliantly there. Which was just as well, for his political convictions would probably have led him to favor independence for Algeria. With the least possible damage, naturally, to the image of France. . . .

And now Saffie, a German, was sitting right in front of that same living-room window. And no one had sat in this living room in quite the way she was sitting there since it had first been built in the middle of the seventeenth century. No one.

Her thick painted lips smile fixedly; her large green eyes rest on Raphael in calm expectancy.

Raphael is so overwhelmed by her presence that he's almost forgotten the reason for it. Rising, he starts to pace the room, running his left hand over and over through his hair, backward from forehead to crown, with fingers spread. This feverish artistic gesture has been a habit with him since adolescence, but it's growing faintly ludicrous because his black curls are receding farther and farther on his forehead — yes, the fact of the matter is that at age twenty-eight Raphael Lepage is prematurely bald, so that now, for fully three quarters of its trajectory, his left hand meets nothing but naked skin.

Even as he thus paces the room and runs his hand over his balding head, Raphael is holding forth. He describes the tasks and responsibilities that will be those of the young woman he hires as a maid. To tell the truth, he's not particularly conversant in domestic matters and is spouting information virtually at random, grasping at whatever memories of Maria-Felice come to mind — Maria-Felice standing on a stepladder to wash the windowpanes, Maria-Felice bringing him his mail and breakfast at nine in the morning and his tea at five in the afternoon, Maria-Felice going out to do the food shopping, serving bowls of soup, struggling up the back staircase with a heavy bag of logs for the fireplace. . . . Raphael summarizes all this as best he can, illustrating with gestures and pantomime, glancing at the young woman now and then to make certain she is following. She appears to be. Yes, she seems to know what he means, but then . . . it would seem she knows everything about the world there is to know, and always has.

He tells her he's a professional flutist, a member of an orchestra (he articulates the orchestra's name with care but Saffie doesn't blink, her eyebrows don't go up, her mouth doesn't drop open — clearly she's never heard of it). He adds that he's frequently away on trips, that his absences are sometimes short (concerts in the provinces) and sometimes long (tours abroad); that Saffie's duties during these periods will naturally be fewer, but that she can take advantage of her free time (does she understand the word "advantage"?) to — oh — to polish the silver, for example.

Her room's on the seventh floor. Visitors strictly forbidden. He realizes that he's now speaking in the indicative, as if they'd already reached an agreement on the subject of her working hours, her wages, the very fact that it is she, Saffie, who will be taking this job — that, starting tomorrow morning and for the foreseeable future, it is she, this strange and silent young German woman, who will be looking after him, Raphael Lepage, a flutist on the verge of becoming famous, in his large apartment on the Rue de Seine, dusting his books, putting sugar in his tea, ironing his shirts, washing his underwear, and changing the sheets after his lovers leave his bed.

"Do we have an agreement?"

Slowly, she nods her head.

"Where are your things?"

"Not many things. Two suitcases only. I go get them now?"

Good Lord, her voice. He hadn't noticed it before. A devastatingly fragile voice. It paralyzes him. He needs to make a conscious effort to stop standing there staring at her like an idiot. And another effort to grasp, in an inward echo, the meaning of the words she's just spoken.

II

Saffie's suitcases are at the Young Women's Hostel on the Boulevard Saint Michel, where the windows of her room look out onto the Luxembourg Gardens. It isn't very far from Raphael Lepage's apartment to the Young Women's Hostel — as a matter of fact it's a perfectly delightful walk. The Rue de Seine begins (as its name suggests) at the river Seine and, after changing its name to the Rue de Tournon, extends all the way to the Luxembourg Palace, home of the Senate of this fine country to which Saffie has just emigrated. The street widens imperceptibly along its final hundred yards, giving a deceptive impression of perfect parallels to those who contemplate the Senate from the Boulevard Saint Germain. Naturally, Saffie can't be expected to notice this. She might, on the other hand, glance around her from time to time as she walks up the street. On either side are art galleries, antique shops, cafes filled to overflowing with creative individuals who are lighting up cigarettes and exhaling peremptory political and literary opinions along with the smoke, store windows cluttered with Japanese prints, ancient globes, Persian rugs . . . So many things that might arouse her curiosity! No, she walks on at an even pace, neither hurrying nor dawdling, staring straight ahead of her and seeing nothing. She doesn't attract people's attention. She doesn't turn the heads of the young and not so young men sitting on the terrace of *La Palette*. It's as if she were invisible — a ghost. And yet she's quite real; she knows the rules that govern human behavior in cities; she stops at the red light, for instance, before crossing the boulevard.

Skirting the Senate, she enters the vast Luxembourg Gardens — just now in full bloom and blossom, bursting with petals and poetry and poignancy. Her features neutral, her eyes glassy, she walks past the marble statues and the fountains, past the little boys steering their little boats across the water, the palm trees just recently brought out of the greenhouses in which they've spent the winter, the linden trees with their brand new leaves, the cafés set up in their dappled shadow, and the Medicis Fountain, on either side of which young university students, in chairs they've paid to sit in, are passionately absorbed in reading Jean-Paul Sartre or kissing one other, with considerable involvement of the tongue. She doesn't slip behind the fountain to contemplate, heart aflutter, the blueing bronze haut-relief of Leda being triumphantly raped by the god of gods who's metamorphosed into a swan.

She's already seen it. Saffie has seen it all.

Coming out of the park onto the Boulevard Saint Michel, she walks into the hostel, goes directly over to the reception desk, pays for the nights she's spent there, climbs to the second floor to fetch her suitcases — and finally, leaving the key at the desk, takes exactly the same route back across the park, her face as impassive as before.

Incredible as it may seem, Raphael is watching for her from the little balcony. He hasn't gone back to practicing Marin Marais. His flute is lying right where he left it, on the blue velvet of its open case. As a rule, he takes fanatical care of his instrument — if you don't wipe out the inside with a rag after each use, the drops of saliva formed by your condensed breath can corrode the metal and the pads, eventually causing rust and rot. But today's already a holiday in Raphael's heart — he's inexplicably overjoyed that this young, impenetrable woman will be coming to live beneath his roof — and so he stands there on the little window balcony, watching for her, not even bothering to conceal himself, obsessed with the idea that she might not come back at all, that she might vanish as mysteriously as she appeared . . . or that he might have imagined her entire visit.

He isn't telling himself, "You must be crazy. A maid . . . of all things . . ." No. He isn't trying to minimize the absurd importance this foreign woman has just taken on in his life. That's love for you.

At last he catches sight of her, carrying a heavy suitcase in each hand, her pace now jerky and laborious — and gives a start, aghast. Why hadn't he offered to go with her, or at least to hire her a taxi? It hadn't occurred to him that she might carry her luggage all the way back on foot. Cursing himself under his breath, he flies down the staircase and dashes out to meet her in the street. He can't help himself. That's love for you.

"Saffie!" he cries, coming up to her.

He knows he'll have to hide his love — and for a good while, too, so as not to put her off, scare her, give her a pretext for taking to her heels. He'll treat her with kindness and courtesy, he decides, taking care to preserve the dignity and distance appropriate to an employer-employee relationship.

"I'm sorry — how stupid of me! I should have gotten you a taxi . . . I hope you're not too exhausted? Especially in this heat . . ."

Setting down her suitcases on the Rue de Seine's busy sidewalk, Saffie looks at Raphael. Really looks at him for the first time. Perhaps she hasn't understood what he just said? Yes, she has . . . No, she hasn't . . . Abruptly, she bursts out laughing. On the terrace of *La Palette,* people turn to look at her, at them, and Raphael stiffens — he hates making a show of himself involuntarily. Saffie's laughter is loud and ferocious — and then it stops. She vanishes once again behind her pale mask, her artificial smile.

"It's nothing," she says.

And picks up the suitcases again. But, at Raphael's insistence, hands him one of them.

The elevator, only recently constructed in the stairwell of this elegant old building, is barely large enough for two adults with two suitcases. Raphael is aroused to find himself in such confined quarters with Saffie; her presence-absence is so close he can almost touch it. He smells her perfume and her body fluids, sees the way her blouse is sticking to her skin with sweat, guesses at the shape of her breasts, then lowers his eyes to stop looking at her for he has a throbbing, almost painful erection. . . . Meanwhile, for the fifty long and lovely palpitating seconds that separate the ground floor from the seventh floor, Saffie is somewhere else.

In reality, the elevator only goes to the sixth floor and they must climb up to the seventh, where the maids' rooms are. Raphael purposely precedes Saffie on the staircase, so as not to torture himself by watching the way her body moves beneath her pleated skirt.

His self-possession is remarkable. As he takes out the key to open the door of her room, then shows her the Turkish-style toilets she'll be sharing with the other tenants on the floor, and the tiny sink at the end of the hall with its cold water tap and cracked mirror, neither his hands nor his voice tremble. Like all performers, he's developed solid techniques for mastering his nerves. Deep breathing, relaxation, intense concentration on an object, a smell, or a sensation having no connection with the threatening element of a given situation . . . Raphael Lepage is past master of self-control. Every breath, every muscle, virtually every particle of his body obeys the orders of his brain.

He knows how to be patient.

Containing his strength only makes him more aware of it.

He's an exceptionally mature young man.

.   .   .   .   .   .

Saffie looks at everything Raphael shows her, saying little but nodding every now and then to show she understands.

"So, does that sound all right?"

At last he mentions a figure — a rather pitiful monthly salary, to be honest, even taking into account the fact that she'll be getting room and board — and grins at her, unabashed.

"That sounds all right," says Saffie at once.

Raphael looks deep into her eyes and comes up against the wall of jade. Drawing an elegant pocket watch from his trousers (the only one of his father's personal effects he'd cared to keep for himself), he exclaims, feigning surprise, "But . . . it's nearly one o'clock, you must be dying of hunger!"

"Dying, no . . ." says Saffie.

"Hahaha!" laughs Raphael, not sure if she's joking. "Just a manner of speaking," he adds.

To this she makes no answer.

"What I meant is, are you hungry?"

"Yes."

"Well, then, come on downstairs. I'll show you around the kitchen and we can have a bite to eat together — that will be one thing out of the way."

"A bite?"

What's gotten into him, suggesting having lunch with the maid, barely two hours after having met her? He can't imagine. And, like the fact of not having wiped down his flute, this gives him a pleasant sensation of dizziness. If his mother could see him now. . . . Well, his mother had befriended Maria-Felice, hadn't she? And the two women often had meals together, didn't they? He doesn't see the difference.

He does see the difference.

Once again, in quick succession: elevator, erection, relaxation, a steady hand turning the key in the lock. As they move around the kitchen, Raphael sprinkles his explanations with little jokes and stories to put Saffie at ease. He gives her the rundown on the stove (gas flame, here's where the matches are kept), the nearest market (the Rue de Buci), and her new employer's tastes in food (he's fond of fish, loathes cabbage and cauliflower, has a weakness for berry tarts).

"What sort of cooking do you like to do? Do you make German dishes?"

"German . . . dishes?" repeats Saffie, as if this were an expression devoid of meaning. And Raphael guffaws, elated by what he thinks must be the bond springing up between them.

"You're right, the Germans haven't invented much in the way of cuisine, have they? Apart from sauerkraut — and *that,* like everything to do with cabbage, I can't stand!"

Saffie's fixed smile trembles a little. Does she mean to convey that *she's* not crazy about sauerkraut either? Still, she hasn't yet given him the slightest clue about what she can cook.

Well, he'll find out soon enough.

Meanwhile, he takes some eggs and a head of romaine lettuce from the refrigerator. Shows Saffie the cupboards in which, since long before his birth, the condiments and spices, oils and vinegars, plates and glasses, cutlery and saucepans have been kept . . . and politely requests that she call him when lunch is ready.

At this point, Saffie asks her first question.

"Have you a . . ." she says. "A? . . ."

She gestures to make up for the missing word. Raphael takes a clean apron from a drawer and hands it to her, repressing the incongruous impulse to tie it around her waist.

"Apron," he murmurs. "It's called an apron."

"Yes," says Saffie. "Apron. I was thinking napkin. Apron. I was confusing."

"See you later."

"Yes."

The lunch is faultless.

Salad dressing with the perfect ratio of vinegar to oil, eggs fried so that the whites are congealed but not the yolks, baguette sliced at a sharp angle, blue napkins folded into triangles to the left of the plates, crystal glasses and carafe . . . Faultless, though Saffie would likely have been unable to name half the objects on the table.

"Thank you," says Raphael, sitting down.

He eats heartily, his head still dancing to the *Folies d'Espagne* he'd gone over again while waiting for lunch to be ready — he'll be playing it in public the day after tomorrow. Watching Saffie eat, he sees that in spite of her scrawniness she has a good appetite. Knows how to use bread to wipe her plate clean. Chews and swallows diligently, leaving not a crumb behind.

But . . . it's like all the rest. He's convinced that she tastes nothing of what she eats. And that at the end of the meal, she'd be unable to say — even in German — what she just swallowed. She wipes her lips on a corner of the blue napkin, her gaze vacant.

Raphael has no inclination to ask her the usual questions. He doesn't want to make small talk with her. Love, yes. But — where are you from, where did you learn French, how long are you planning to stay in Paris — no. He's excited by the singularity of the situation. Excited to find himself alone in his own house with a young green-eyed foreigner who says practically nothing. He venerates her silence.

Saffie gets up without a word, puts on the apron she'd removed before the meal, clears the table and starts washing up.

"I have to go out," Raphael announces.

She nods indifferently.

"So — well — here are the keys."

If his mother could see him! Handing over the keys of *her* apartment, the large and beautiful Trala family apartment on the Rue de Seine, to a German.

"This one's the key to your room. . . . This one's for the back entrance. . . . And this is for the wine cellar. Do you like good wine?"

"Yes."

Fabulous. The way she never adds anything. Never obfuscates her meaning with formulas of hollow courtesy, frivolous embellishment, neurotic commentary: Do you like good wine? Yes. Incredible, thinks Raphael, how virtually everything people say in the course of a day is superfluous.

"Good!" he says out loud. "Well, I'm off then. Get yourself settled, rest up as much as you like, I'll be eating out this evening.

Tomorrow I'll show you where things are kept, for the house-cleaning. Is that okay with you?"

"Yes, that's okay with me . . . okay . . . with me."

She repeats the phrase slowly, in a low voice. Perhaps she's never heard it before?

"So, see you soon."

"So, see you soon," she echoes, this time with a real smile on her face. Hm, that *was* rather catchy, wasn't it?

"So see you soon so see you soon," murmurs Raphael a few minutes later, as he knots his tie in front of the bedroom mirror.

And he goes out.

A true wonder. A woman in your own home, a woman you pay, and to whom you owe no explanations. Mama in Burgundy for good. No one around to coddle him, watch over him, ask him what his plans are for the day . . . or for the night.

Is she a virgin? wonders Raphael, arriving at the Odéon intersection and plunging down the stairs into the metro. Surely not, if I'm any judge of women. Looks as if she's seen her share of life. But love? he goes on dreamily, unfolding the *Monde* he's just purchased at the newsstand. No, I doubt it. I'd be very surprised if she knew much about love. Very surprised indeed.

III

Saffie's in her room under the eaves. She's unpacked her suitcases, which contain everything she owns in the world.

Almost all of it is clothing, and only one item of clothing is worth describing at any length — the uniform she stole from the Welcome Hostesses School just before she left Düsseldorf, telling herself, You never know, a little style can always come in handy. And indeed the uniform is very chic: it consists of a round, flat, inordinately wide black hat (something like two feet across), a slinky black shoulderless dress, black lace gloves, and three fat white bunches of faux-pearl grapes (a brooch and two earrings).

In Düsseldorf the month before, despite this highly flattering outfit and despite the generally satisfactory raw material she represented, Saffie had failed to make an impression in the role of Welcome Hostess. The instructors had patiently explained what was expected of her: a smile, discretion, cool seductiveness, imperturbable courtesy, walking on stiletto heels without wiggling her rear end . . . but to no avail. During the role-playing sessions in which she was supposed to welcome the "clients" — ostensibly businessmen newly arrived in town for a convention (automobile, life insurance, hotel management, Ideal Home . . .) — she'd stand there smiling fixedly, a pen in one black-gloved hand and an official document in the other . . . and when the time came, she could never quite manage to come to life, move smoothly and animatedly, transform the exercise into something meaningful. Her superiors, who were playing the clients, while agreeing that the young woman had charm, were forced to admit that given their objectives (economic miracle and *tutti quanti*), her performance was simply not good enough. Thus, they'd dismissed her gently and given her a month's salary by way of compensation, much of which she'd used on the spot to buy a one-way train ticket to Paris. Then, noticing that one of her suitcases was just wide enough (twenty-six inches) for the black hat, she'd decided not to give her elegant uniform back to the school.

What else is in her suitcases?

Her mother's missal, which she hasn't opened in the twelve years since her mother died.

A heavy woolen blanket, in the event she might be reduced to sleeping on park benches.

A pair of fur-lined boots.

A good gray woolen winter coat.

A stuffed gray poodle paw — all that remains of the toy that had kept her company throughout her childhood. The poodle had protected her from nightmares as long as this was possible — that is, until her father's death. Now it is no longer possible, but she keeps the paw with her out of loyalty. Both her parents are dead and she's severed all ties with her brothers and sisters, but her loyalty to the poodle leg is unshakeable.

There. Saffie has now put everything away, it's still only four o'clock in the afternoon and she's got nothing to do until tomorrow morning. She lies down on her bed and stares at the ceiling. Doesn't fall asleep. Doesn't read a book. Doesn't daydream. After a while she gets up again, goes out to the toilets on the landing and all but vomits. Germans will never understand how the French manage to combine the sublime and the ignoble, philosophy and pissotières, the most scintillating spiritual creations and the most revolting bodily waste.

She goes down to the empty apartment on the third floor, rummages around under the sink, finds a scrubbing brush and some Ajax, a pail and a rag, and goes back up to the seventh floor to clean the squat-down toilets. Holding her breath and gritting her teeth, she furiously scrubs at the excrements of a dozen strangers, her fellow tenants. She has no choice. She can't do otherwise. When she's finished, she returns to her room and lies back down on the bed, eyes open wide. Stares at the ceiling.

Raphael's day, meanwhile, has been equally devoid of novelistic events. He's gone to a rehearsal. For three and a half hours, the orchestra went over pieces by Bach and Ibert — and then, since Raphael was in unusually good form, he played the Marin Marais for them. His circular breathing was functioning beautifully. . . .

Raphael can play the flute almost indefinitely, without stopping for breath, because he knows how to inhale through his nostrils and exhale through his mouth at the same time. It's a dauntingly difficult technique (few musicians have ever mastered it; even Rampal had to give up trying), but Raphael has spent ten long years perfecting it. Every time he would get bored — listening to his mother's unending litany of complaints, for instance, or sitting through music theory classes at the Conservatory — he would concentrate on his breathing.

Before the war, Monsieur Lepage senior had taught his young son to play chess while describing to him the most thrilling episodes of the French Revolution — he'd recite Robespierre's impassioned speeches verbatim, paint vivid pictures of the executioner sharpening the guillotine's blade, crowds pouring into the Place de Grève, heads dropping into the basket with a thud — the basket filled to overflowing by day's end with wild-haired bloody heads, the eyes staring madly at nothing. . . . "Checkmate, son!" he'd invariably conclude, with a triumphant chuckle.

This was how Raphael had learned to do two things at once, coordinating them while keeping them separate in his mind. It's a highly singular talent. In addition to circular breathing, it enables him to balance his budget while talking to a friend over the telephone, or to check out the charms of a new romantic interest while indulging in a piece of raspberry pie.

His solo drew cries of admiration from the other musicians, secretly thrilling Raphael. (Raphael loves to be loved, he delights in mesmerizing his public, taking them by the hand and leading them out of this world; "The Pied Piper" has been his favorite story ever since he was a boy.) Toward the end of the afternoon, he decided to take a few minutes to enjoy the fine weather and stroll down by the used-book stalls lining the Seine across from Notre Dame Cathedral. He stopped off at his favorite music stores, symmetrically located on either side of the Place Saint Michel. Then he went up to the seventeenth arrondissement to have dinner with a trombonist friend and his family, after which the two young men ambled down to a bar in the Place Clichy for a couple of a whiskies. Raphael lent a sympathetic ear to his friend's financial worries —

all the while following, with his other ear, a tumultuous conversation at the next table concerning the "events" in Algeria. (National Liberation Front fighters, as part of their quarrel with the National Algerian Movement fighters, have just slit the throats, chopped off the arms, legs, and heads of two hundred and fifty people in the town of Melouza — including women, children, and the elderly. In response, two hundred and fifty Algerians from the Melouza region have decided to become harkis, joining the French army in its effort to put down their own people.)

It's nearly two in the morning when Raphael gets back to the Rue de Seine. Looking up at the top floor, he sees that the light is still on in Saffie's attic window. This surprises him — and, for a moment, his heart beats a little faster.

Saffie is an excellent maid in every way. Her cooking is simple but tasty, and her uniform — tight black skirt, white blouse and apron — is always immaculate. She says, "Yes, Sir," "No, Sir," "Good evening, Sir," and never forgets to smile. She cleans the house thoroughly and noiselessly. She takes advantage of Raphael's absences to make the rounds of the apartment with the vacuum cleaner, that extraordinary invention bestowed by the Second World War upon those who survived it, permitting them to clean rugs without having to shake them out the window.

Slowly the days drift by, and the month of June arrives. Yes, it happens one day in early June.

That evening, too, Raphael gets home around two in the morning, a little drunk. That evening, too, he notices that the light is on in Saffie's room. Doesn't the girl ever sleep? he wonders. Every day she's up and dressed by seven forty-five, when she knocks on his bedroom door to bring him his breakfast.

His integrity and good faith having now been firmly established, Raphael decides it's time to let a bit of curiosity show through.

"Do you go to bed late," he asks Saffie the next morning with a smile, "or do you sleep with the lights on?"

Saffie's jade eyes flash with indignation, almost hatred. She turns away without a word, but her brief display of anger has aroused her employer. Sitting up in bed, he stretches out a hand and gently grasps the fleshiest part of Saffie's not-very-fleshy naked arm, just below the short sleeve of her white blouse.

Saffie freezes.

She freezes, not like someone who's terrified, but rather like someone who knows what's in store for her. This new form of immobility is not unlike that which characterizes her the rest of the time. As usual, scarcely any differently than usual, her body and her entire being seem to be in a state of suspended animation.

And it happens. Raphael draws her gently toward him and sits her down on the edge of the bed — she offers no resistance. He lowers her until she's lying on her back and removes the rubber band from her ponytail, so that her hair spreads out across the sheet covering his thighs — she doesn't so much as bat an eyelash. Softly, very softly, he says her name.

"Saffie."

He knows she must be feeling his erection swell and harden through the sheet at the nape of her neck, but she neither sits up nor turns toward him.

"Saffie," repeats Raphael, thrilled by the contact of her skin and by the astounding lightness of her body lying across his legs. One by one, adagio, adagio, he undoes the buttons of her blouse. Then he turns her over and props her up on her knees. She stays that way.

He doesn't want to take her clothes off; he wants to make love to her in her uniform. As he hitches up her tight black skirt, his movements are somewhat rougher than before but still not violent, betraying only the urgency of desire; his member is now stiff and throbbing and he's controlling it, yes, he knows how to control the unfolding of love's rites and how to elicit as much beauty as possible from them — just as the orchestra modulates the dynamics in the performance of a symphony, not attacking the fortissimo outright but achieving it *poco a poco,* so that the paroxysm becomes the natural, ineluctable, incomparable culmination of the crescendo.

Saffie is wearing nylon stockings and a garter belt; her thighs beneath his palms are thin and taut.

"Oh, Saffie, oh Saffie," repeats Raphael, now breathing into her ear. "I've wanted you since the first time I saw you. . . ."

She says nothing. He starts breathing faster, still whispering into her ear, curving his body around the curve of her back. Without removing her panties, he pulls their silky material aside with two fingers — and enters her with a grand, magnificent slowness. She in no way seeks to free herself from his embrace — it's not the first time, that much is clear, she knows what's going on — and he moves inside her with long repeated moans (Gluck, "Triomphi amor") — holding back, holding back, then not holding back anymore, allowing himself to be carried away by the torrent, crying out her name, giving now, giving, all but dissolving into tears at the end so utterly has he given of himself, more perhaps than ever in his life before, with any prostitute, with any great or not so great love, ever.

Saffie has already moved away. Getting to her feet, she adjusts her clothing in front of the wardrobe mirror — a mirror she cleans weekly, every Friday morning. She can see her reflection in the glass — and behind her, in the disorder of the sheets, sprawled flat on his back with his arms and legs flung wide, the individual with dark curls and a premature bald spot. She knows his name, what his clothes smell like before and after washing, what food he likes to eat; now she also knows his nudity, and the deep groans that emerge from his throat at the height of his pleasure.

With a certain satisfaction, she notes that there's not a single streak on the whole surface of the mirror.

Raphael goes out for the rest of the morning. At lunchtime, Saffie serves him an egg-and-tuna-fish salad and gives him his phone messages. As if nothing at all had happened between them.

He's crazy about her.

He has a concert that same evening and performs sublimely, obsessed with the thought of Saffie from the orchestra's first tune-up to the audience's last handclap. Upon arriving home and seeing that her light is on, he goes up to the seventh floor and scratches at her door like a cat. She lets him in without a word. She's dressed for bed — in a baggy white cotton nightgown, yellow from re-peated washings.

This time he undresses her.

He, too, undresses — and, standing next to her in the stifling heat, seeks out her eyes. Raphael is a very handsome man. And his love is as sincere as any other. He's not marveling at finding him-self alone with the maid in the maid's room. He genuinely hopes to awaken this strange young woman's desire — or, at the very least, to capture her attention. Before possessing her a second time, he longs to make her look at *him,* smile at *him* — as a person. They're standing face to face, their naked bodies brushing inter-mittently, and he's erect — but rather than pressing her to him, he bends to catch her lips between his own and wet them with his tongue. Like all flutists, his lips and tongue are sensitive, subtle, savvy.

Saffie lets it happen.

Raphael sees that she has no intention of resisting. Him or anyone else. She'll let it happen, always. Whatever a man wants to do to her body — kiss it, undress it, push, bite, twist, bind, gag, beat, kill it — she'll let it happen. An image flashes into Raphael's mind, from a photography exhibit he saw in a neighborhood gallery some time ago — Hans Bellmer's doll, trussed and tied, dismembered and reassembled, her limbs juxtaposed any which way, forever smiling, neutral, icily indifferent.

Dear Lord, what can have happened to her?

Though they're standing motionless, their skin is already smooth and slick with sweat.

Raphael sets his hands on Saffie's narrow hips. Slowly, he kneels in front of her and breathes in her scent. With infinite delicacy, his tongue begins to explore her. His hands move amorously from the young woman's hips to her buttocks. And Saffie, in the suffocating humid heat of this garret room in Paris, observes what's happening from a distance. As if it were happening in a mirror, or in a film. This person's half-bald head moving around down there. The silky black curls. The sound of air squelching in and out, the sound of mucous membranes touching, the sound of spit. She has no idea who this man is, who this woman is, why anything. Suddenly weak, she rocks on her feet and Raphael rises in alarm. Catches her in his arms. Carries her over to the bed.

Lying down beside her, he breathes cool air over her face.

"Breath is so wonderful," he tells her in a low voice. "It can do anything. When you're cold it warms you and when you're hot it cools you. . . . Are you all right now?"

"Yes," says Saffie. "It is so hot."

The mere sound of her voice makes him hard again. They are lying side by side on the narrow bed, naked and drenched in sweat. He makes love to her. They don't make love with each other — no, far from it; Raphael makes love to Saffie.

And, just as he had that morning, he gives of himself without reserve, coming and coming, overwhelmed by love. Saffie's eyes are closed or open, it makes no difference. Her body isn't inert, it's absent. Static, even when it moves.

Raphael discovers he hasn't the least wish to get up and go back downstairs. For the first time in his life, he feels that beauty and necessity are converging in his heart, as they do in a Bach fugue.

"Saffie, . . ." he whispers hesitantly, fearing that she might laugh at him, after what has just transpired between them twice in the same day — "I want to use *tu* when I speak to you."

After a brief silence, she replies, also in a whisper, "And me too?"

"Oh, yes! Yes, of course, you too."

"*Tu*," says Saffie slowly, as if to taste the expression on her tongue.

"And . . . and not only that," Raphael goes on ardently, urgently, still in a whisper, "but I want . . . I want you . . . to come and sleep downstairs. It's too hot up here."

"Sleep where?"

"In my bed. With me. If you want to. Do you want to?"

This time there's a long silence, during which Raphael feels his heart beating erratically. He's keenly aware of the fact that he is plunging headlong into something highly abnormal.

Still Saffie makes no answer.

So Raphael says something stranger still, his heart beating so wildly that he can scarcely hear the words as they fall from his own lips.

He says, "I want you to marry me, Saffie."

Saffie remains silent. Sick with love, he insists, "Do you understand?" And reiterates, very slowly, articulating every syllable, "I want you to be my wife."

Silence. And then — "That's okay with me," says Saffie.

Without looking at him, without smiling: the expression he taught her on the day they first met. That's okay with me.

IV

When her son calls to announce his intention to be lawfully united in marriage with the German woman he recently hired as a maid, Hortense Trala-Lepage almost sinks into a swoon.

For four full years, in the city of Paris occupied by the Germans, Hortense had endured the consummate torture of food shortages. Though the family fortune by the end of the depression-wracked thirties was no longer what it had been at the turn of the century, when Grandpa Trala began reaping the first profits from his Algerian vineyards, the Trala-Lepages were far from destitute. The problem was that there was no food to be bought, particularly in the wintertime. And what food there was turned out to be of such poor quality that it was thoroughly humiliating, for a woman who took pride in giving her maid precise and inventive instructions on gastronomical matters.

Two pounds of potatoes per person per fortnight. Fifty grams of butter a month. Apart from that: rutabaga and kohlrabi, celeriac and Jerusalem artichokes. The names of these vegetables might have an exotic ring, but they could hardly fill a man's stomach. Not even a child's. Day after day, the same depressing signs sprouted in the store windows: "No Meat," "No Bread," "No Milk." On the Rue de Seine, the Trala-Lepages had known hunger. Not only that, but — "No Coal" — they'd known cold. Raphael's mother has never forgotten. One morning, in the month of December 1941, they'd been reduced to burning some old chairs and a wooden trunk to keep warm.

There was the humiliation of hunger, the humiliation of cold — and also the supreme, unforgettable humiliation of bomb alerts, when one had to scramble down to the cellar in one's nightdress and wait there for hours, rubbing up against the bodies and inhaling the odors of people one did not so much as greet when one passed them in the staircase. Flabby women trying desperately to knit with trembling hands; men whittling nervously away at pieces of wood like soldiers in trenches. And Raphael, their angel — their darling angel Raphael, aged twelve, then thirteen, sweetly playing the flute in a corner of the shelter to calm the others, take their minds off their fear . . .

All of this — the food lines, the hunger and the cold, the degrading lack of privacy during bomb alerts, to say nothing of the tragic death of Monsieur Lepage senior — had been the Germans' fault.

What, indeed, did Raphael know about this woman, this . . . whatever her name was? A ludicrous-sounding name. How could he have gotten to know her in such a short time? And go so far as to put his life into her hands? Where had this Zaffie been during the war? Yes, of course, she was only a child at the time, I realize that. But what about her parents? Had she told Raphael anything about her parents?

"They're both deceased, Mother."

"*Now* they're deceased, very well. But were they deceased *then*, during the war?"

"No."

"And do you know what they were? Whether they were favorable to that . . . abominable regime?"

"No."

"Ah! You see?"

Her tone is jubilant. As if she'd won the first round.

"What do I see?"

"I mean . . . maybe they were . . . maybe they did . . ."

"My dear, dear Mother . . ." Holding the receiver in his right hand, Raphael runs the fingers of his left hand through the absent curls on the top of his head. "I hope you don't mean to suggest that guilt is hereditary?"

"No, no, it isn't that . . ."

"Or that Saffie has inherited some . . . I don't know, some sort of Teutonic flaw . . . that might predispose her to cruel and unnatural acts? . . . Just what are you insinuating, anyway?"

"I'm not insinuating anything, angel. . . . I'm simply telling you — with all my strength, Raphael, and with all my love for you, and with all my hopes for your fulfillment in your life and work — *not to do it! Please* listen to me! *Please* trust me! I'm your mother! It's madness!"

Seated at her writing desk in the blue room on the third floor of her quasi-castle in Burgundy, Hortense Trala-Lepage bursts into tears.

"What on earth is going on?" says Raphael. "Is my little 'Mammoth' really as upset as all that? Listen, Ma, don't forget that I'm a flutist, and that for the past two centuries the flute has been the emblem of friendship between France and Germany! Think of

Johann Joachim Quantz, who invented the E-flat key — he was a collector of French painting! Voltaire himself went to visit him in his castle at Sans-Souci!"

Hortense's sobbing only gets louder. An explosive sound comes through the receiver, and Raphael wonders if it's a sneeze or the sarcastic repetition of the name "Sans-Souci."

"Think of Theobald Böhm," he goes on. "What would my life be like without the Böhm flute? And where did he choose to take out a patent for it? In Paris, Mother! At the Paris Academy of Science!"

Still no coherent answer at the other end of the line; nothing but a savage series of sniffs and snorts.

After hanging up, Raphael remains standing in the hallway for a moment, pensive and annoyed. He hadn't foreseen such a violent reaction on his mother's part, and it bothers him more than he likes to admit. Independence is all well and good; still, you'd think a mother would want to attend her own son's wedding.

But Madame Trala-Lepage sticks to her principles. Not only does she refuse to come to Paris for the ceremony itself, she categorically and definitively refuses to meet her daughter-in-law.

Despite this cruel decision, Raphael refuses to feel dejected. Something in him wants to be happy, he's made that way — and moreover, he knows it's up to him to teach happiness to Saffie.

Where is Saffie, anyway?

He finds her on all fours, her hands encased in rubber gloves, washing the kitchen floor. Since their engagement she's stopped wearing a uniform, but she continues to do the housework with the same perfectionism and the same absent smile on her face. . . .

He stares at her. All of a sudden he finds her a bit frightening.

"You'll be magnificent on our wedding day!" he says, to reassure himself.

"Yes," she replies, getting to her feet. "I already have a dress." To his surprise, she trots off to the bedroom to change.

Reappears wearing the stylish uniform of the Düsseldorf Welcome Hostesses School.

Raphael shudders. The sight of Saffie in her black vamp getup makes his blood run cold.

"No," he says. "Let me buy you a beautiful white gown. It would make me so happy! Why would you want to wear black? It's not a funeral, you know!"

"Yes, it is!" she retorts, a mischievous gleam in her eyes. "You tell me you bury your bachelorhood, so I wear mourning for it!"

Raphael bursts out laughing (hmm, the young lady's already learning to make jokes in French!) and gives in. He's mad about her. Taking her in his arms, he kisses the nape of her neck over and over, licks and nibbles at her naked shoulders, then patiently goes about undoing the ribbons and hooks and zippers that keep this black dress attached to the body of the woman he loves. . . .

Okay, that's all well and good, but now it's time to move on to more serious matters. Saffie's a minor; she's a foreigner; apart from her passport she owns nothing at all in the way of official documents, no formal proof that she's alone in the world, free of parental authority, an orphan. In 1957, French civil servants take this sort of thing very seriously indeed. They insist that one present original, notarized documents, along with photographs of certain specified dimensions, neither a millimeter more nor a millimeter less, full face and not three-quarters, with a background that is gray not white, or white not gray, and every single paper in one's file must be signed and countersigned, stamped and counterstamped in six or seven different offices.

(Nowadays, of course, all this has changed radically. The employees of Paris town halls and police stations no longer treat people with the condescension, arrogance, and malevolence for which they were once famous. Nowadays, the minute you set foot in a Paris administrative service, you enter into a state not far from ecstasy. The walls of the waiting room are covered with gaily-colored frescoes of joyfully leaping figures. All the employees have made love that very morning; their faces are still tender and touched; they stare at you moist-eyed and listen to your problems with the deepest sympathy — following which they beg you to make yourself comfortable in a plush armchair, hand you a masterpiece of world literature to pass the time, something by Anton Chekhov or Carson McCullers, for example — and then, by Jove, they get down to those problems of yours and they get them solved.)

Fearlessly, Raphael devotes himself to the task. From the day he was born, his mother's family money and his father's libertarian philosophy have given him an unshakeable confidence in himself. He knows his rights — and if by chance one of them happens to be missing, he can afford to buy it. Thus, he accompanies Saffie to the town hall and escorts her from office to office, filling out forms and striking up conversations with the sullen, scowling employees, loosening their turgid tongues and cracking their masks of boredom.

To get what one wants in this sort of situation, one has to have a virtually miraculous combination of cards in one's hand (French nationality, white skin, personal charm, financial charisma, convincing threats about friends in high places, and so forth). Raphael Lepage has all these cards and knows what order to play them in; thus, scarcely a fortnight after he first set foot in the bureaucratic maze, his marriage with Saffie can be celebrated in the town hall of Paris's sixth arrondissement, on the Place Saint Sulpice.

June 21, the summer solstice. On this day, though she doesn't know it yet, Saffie is already carrying Raphael's child. She's scarcely a week into pregnancy — her menstrual cycle hasn't been affected yet — so when she dashes into the bathroom to vomit on the morning of their wedding day, Raphael is perplexed.

June 21, 1957 is a fine day. Not as hot as the day, a mere three weeks earlier, on which Raphael and Saffie's bodies joined for the first time. A delightful morning, and the town hall is inundated with sunlight — its blond pinewood floors, banisters, and railings are fairly singing in the rays of gold — it's hard to believe that this is the same building in which Raphael has been rushing about for the past two weeks, deploying all his charm, money, and influence to overcome the mulish resistance of the municipal employees. This morning, the very word "mairie" (town hall), looks like an anagram of "married."

They're married. A simple civic ceremony. No frills, no fuss, no family. Their witnesses are Martin, Raphael's trombonist friend from Clichy, and his wife Michelle. Everyone swears what has to be sworn and signs what has to be signed. The time has come for them to embrace. Raphael's lips graze Saffie's in a pure and shimmering kiss, the tenderest kiss of his whole life, a Debussy kiss, *Prelude to the Afternoon of a Faun*.

Legal matrimony, however, hasn't affected Saffie's lips in the least. They don't express one whit more feeling than they did before she was married.

Now her name is Madame Lepage.

The day after the ceremony, her new family record book in hand, she goes to the West German embassy (ironically located on the Avenue Franklin Roosevelt) and requests a new passport. German civil servants being more efficient than their French counterparts, she receives the document within forty-eight hours. Her old passport is given back to her with one corner snipped off; she immediately tears it to pieces and shoves it into the garbage can.

Her father's name, the family name she bore for the first twenty years of her existence, has been obliterated once and for all.

Might this be the reason for which Saffie replied "okay with me" so readily and so unexpectedly, when Raphael asked her to marry him?

Whether he was acting impulsively or not, whether she had ulterior motives or not, the threads of their destinies are now irrevocably intertwined — since, though neither knows it yet, the young German woman and her French husband are expecting a child. A new human being, the genetic mix of these two highly disparate individuals, is already underway. . . .

There's no turning back. The words they've pronounced, the decisions they've taken, are going to have consequences.

V

Their wedding night in no way differs from the other nights they've spent together in this bed — Raphael makes love to Saffie, then falls asleep. He sleeps like a baby, and there's a touching contrast between the angelic expression on his face and the mature bald spot on his head. His handsome hairy chest, naked on this warm late-June night, moves gently up and down in time to the steady movements of his lungs. Among his numerous other talents, Raphael has the rare virtue of not snoring at all when he sleeps. Thanks to his exceptional breathing abilities, his respiratory tracts are always clear.

Saffie, as usual, stares at the ceiling. She doesn't fall asleep until nearly four in the morning — and even then she sleeps fitfully.

Her spasmodic twitching, however, doesn't disturb her new husband's slumber in the least.

What she doesn't know is that Raphael has set the alarm clock for six in the morning. He's placed it on the night table next to his side of the bed so that he can turn it off at once, before its clamor awakens his bride. His plan is to surprise her by going out to buy croissants at the bakery across the street. For once, he wants to bring Saffie breakfast in bed instead of the other way around. He longs to see her face light up, feel her flesh come to life at the touch of his hands. . . . He knows she doesn't love him — yet — but he's confident that this will change. It's like music, he tells himself. Passion is nothing without patience, diligence, hard work . . . but little by little, it starts to happen. It will happen in their marriage, too. He can't conceive of it not happening. Up until now he's achieved every single goal he's set for himself in life, without exception. This is why he sleeps so well.

Gradually the darkness recedes and the first glimmers of dawn come seeping through the shutters of their bedroom window on the Rue de Seine. (The shutters are closed, but were we to open them we'd see that the window looks out onto an inner courtyard replete with flowerbeds, window boxes, climbing ivy and Virginia creeper; we'd hear pigeons and tits, robins and swallows amorously chirping and cooing . . . so true is it that money enables the inhabitants of the ancient heart of Paris to pretend they live in the country.)

The alarm goes off.

And, instantly, chaos erupts.

Saffie starts to scream, thrashing about in bed with her eyes tightly closed.

Raphael flings his arm out wildly in the direction of the night table and knocks over the alarm clock, which goes flying across the room and crashes to the floor next to the door, all the while continuing to jangle angrily while Saffie continues to scream — a sonorous, high-pitched scream, the scream of a little girl.

Panic-stricken, disoriented, still not fully awake, Raphael fumbles around in the half-light, looking for the goddamn clock. Finds it at last, throttles it — and wheels around.

Saffie is bunched into a tight little ball beneath the sheets.

And Raphael — bewildered. Completely at sea, poor man. He comes over and lays a tentative hand on the ball.

The ball convulses, throws off the sheets and suddenly unwinds, turning into a naked female body that goes leaping into the adjacent bathroom — and pukes its guts out.

Ah . . . A gleam appears in Raphael's eye. He thinks he finally has an inkling of what is going on. (But the alarm clock? The screaming?) Might it be that his wife — his lovely, cherished Saffie — is already pregnant with his child?

Head buzzing with happiness, he sits back down on the bed. Listens to the ticking of the clock. It's a metronome — a hundred and twenty beats per minute — and he uses it to measure the palpitations of his heart. He's going to be a father, he's sure of it. He counts, at once calm and euphoric — yes! His heart is beating nearly as rapidly as the clock! He's going to be a father.

Saffie comes back into the room wearing one of the twelve nightgowns he gave her as a wedding present. The yellow silk makes her pallid skin look almost green.

But she's gotten hold of herself — in fact she's smiling apologetically — and she says,

"I was having a bad dream. I'm sorry. I didn't want to frighten you."

"Don't be sorry," replies Raphael, ruffling her hair. "I've always loved being scared out of my wits! It was like waking up in the middle of the Haunted House at the fun fair! No, seriously though . . . are you all right?"

"Yes, but . . . my stomach is aching me."

"You know what, my little Saffie?" says Raphael, slipping a hand beneath the yellow silk to stroke her belly.

"No . . . ?"

"I was wondering whether . . . your vomiting . . . You wouldn't by any chance be hiding a little Raphael II in there, would you?"

Saffie's greenish face goes white.

"Oh, no," she whispers, and it's clear that what her "Oh, no" signifies is not "I don't think so," but rather "That would be the end of the world."

"My love, my love, my love," murmurs Raphael, pulling her body to him.

Women are happy during pregnancy, he tells himself. They may suffer bouts of nausea during the first weeks because of the upheaval in their hormonal systems, but afterward . . . afterward, they're radiant, resplendent, ravishing. . . . Raphael can't help feeling proud of himself. Not only for having begotten a child, but for having unwittingly stumbled upon this brilliant solution to all of Saffie's problems — motherhood.

Because yes, he does know Saffie has problems. He's neither blind nor stupid. From the first day, from the first minute he set eyes on the young woman standing in the hallway outside his door, he sensed she was marked by some inner wound, a pain so terrible it couldn't be approached head-on. This is why he's always refrained from asking her questions about her childhood. Apart from the death of her parents, he knows nothing of what his wife's existence was like before the day she circled "Seek maid for light housework" in the *Figaro*. But he's optimistic. And determined. And deeply in love. He's convinced that Saffie's mysterious wound will heal gradually under the influence of his love, and that she'll recover the zest for life with which all humans are naturally endowed. What better means to reach this goal than by carrying within her own body, and bringing into the world . . . a new life?

"I set the alarm," explains Raphael, holding Saffie at arm's length and grinning at her. "I thought I'd surprise you by going out to get us some croissants for breakfast."

"It's okay," says Saffie without meeting her husband's gaze. "I'm not hungry."

She turns away and starts to dress.

"No, I can see that!" concedes Raphael. "But darling . . . shouldn't I set up a doctor's appointment for you?"

"Wait a little," says Saffie after a slight hesitation. "Wait for a few days . . . so we are sure."

"All right, my love. As you like. But personally, I'm already sure. I don't know how . . . It must be masculine intuition! I can feel it . . . here!"

Taking Saffie's hand, he lays it on his (naked) testicles. As a joke. But she doesn't laugh.

The newlyweds don't go away for their honeymoon, since Raphael has a contract to spend the month of July on tour in the United States. He's missed a number of rehearsals due to his epic struggle with the many-tentacled French public services, and now he'll have to work hard — both alone and with the orchestra — to catch up. But he'll do it.

During the waiting period she's requested of her husband, the "few days" before her pregnancy becomes official, Saffie throws herself headlong into housework. Single-handedly, she decides to repaint the maid's room. Every day, the minute Raphael's back is turned, she runs up and down the staircase between the third and seventh floors, carrying heavy cans of paint. The neighbors peer out at her through their spy holes, then frown and turn away. Only Mademoiselle Blanche has a foreboding of disaster.

She herself was made sterile in the early fifties from the chemical fumes she involuntarily absorbed at the Wonder Batteries factory of Saint Ouen, where she worked for fifteen long months in the infamous workshop known as "Hell." So when she sees the young woman dashing up and down the stairs instead of taking the elevator, and inhaling oil-based paint and turpentine fumes from morning to night in that tiny room in this scorching heat with all the windows closed . . . she fears the worst.

Mademoiselle Blanche guesses that the girl is pregnant, and it worries her. Does Monsieur Lepage know what his young wife is up to while he's away?

The day Saffie comes up to her — blushing, a German-French dictionary in hand — and asks her where the nearest knitting shop is, Mademoiselle Blanche winces from head to foot and stops guessing. She now knows what's what. There are only two reasons for a woman in the early stages of pregnancy to want to purchase knitting gear — either she's unusually impatient to be a mother, or she doesn't want to be a mother at all. And this young woman . . . well . . . not that the concierge has anything against her, but she just doesn't seem like the type to prepare her layette eight months in advance.

What should I do? wonders Mademoiselle Blanche. Madame Lepage is so distant. My looks probably scare her off. Still, perhaps I could ask her in for a minute when she comes down at noon to pick up the second mail delivery? Offer her a glass of pastis? It's worth a try. . . . There, just like I thought — she refuses, gets flustered, blurts out some excuse and takes to her heels, rushes up the stairs, disappears. Someone else will give her the address of a haberdashery. Perhaps I should have a word with Monsieur Lepage? Concierges are always accused of sticking their noses in other people's business. . . . Still, I should tell him. Tell him what, though? That his wife is expecting a baby? Surely he knows that much. That she's looking for knitting needles? Well, that's not a crime, it's perfectly natural. . . . That I recognize the hunted expression in his young wife's eyes? I used to see it in the eyes of all the new girls, when they came back to the assembly line after their trip to Bordeaux with the boss . . . Mr. Longlegs, his name was, believe it or not . . . all of them had to go through it, and more than once if they were lookers — and then, yes, I remember, some of them. . . .

Now that Mademoiselle Blanche is pouring herself a second glass of pastis and getting lost in her memories, we can tiptoe out of her tacky orange kitchen in which every available surface is cluttered with trinkets and knickknacks and ceramic plates with French monuments painted on them and plants and birdcages and TV schedules and recipes clipped out of *Elle* magazine. . . .

While we were busy drinking pastis with Mademoiselle Blanche, the real drama was taking place — Saffie, bathroom, clothes hanger, white tiles, red blood, Raphael, shouting, telephones, ambulance, hospital, emergency room, nurses, gurney, doctors, examinations, grave discussions, head-shaking . . .

Raphael's cheeks are wet; Saffie's are dry.

Her attempt has failed. The child inside her is still alive. She'll be a mother whether she likes it or not.

She's furious with herself for not having waited until her husband left for the United States — her insomnia, she realizes, sometimes prevents her from thinking clearly.

Raphael entrusts his weak, wan wife to Martin and Michelle, his good friends in Clichy. They're extremely sympathetic, and assure Raphael they'll take the very best care of Saffie. Their eldest daughter is on holiday with cousins at the seaside, and Saffie can have her bedroom. Everything will be just fine, they tell Raphael. Call us whenever you feel like it. Don't worry about a thing. Go play your flute — play like a god.

Raphael is in the plane with the other members of the orchestra. Deeply shaken. Why would she do such a thing? Why, after agreeing to marry him, would she try to kill the child they'd conceived together? Was she afraid pregnancy might deform her body? Or that, having only recently emerged from childhood herself, she mightn't be mature enough to take on the responsibilities of motherhood? Covering his face with his hands, Raphael does his best to concentrate on the chromatic slides in Rimsky-Korsakov's "Flight of the Bumblebee."

Saffie stares at the ceiling. She's lying on the little girl's bed in the little girl's room, its walls papered with clumsy drawings, its furniture covered with dolls. The child on vacation at the seaside is eight years old. Eight, just like Saffie, only not like. Just like Saffie, only not now. Like Saffie when she was eight. Only not like.

She requests that the shutters remain closed from morning to night.

And inside her, day after day, the thing grows.

V I

Let's speed things up here a bit — it's so exhilarating, this power, like in a dream, you can be voluptuously basking in a particular moment and then — ah, the thrill of it — you decide to accelerate and the days go zipping past, rising and falling like waves, dissolving into one other . . . Let's spend a while just floating on the ocean of events that are taking place on the planet Earth in the fall of 1957. We can feel the heavy swell down in the depths. . . . Every now and then, some familiar flotsam and jetsam go bobbing past — Raphael with a loving, solicitous look on his face; Saffie with her gaze perpetually turned inward — but they're caught up by breakers almost at once and sucked under, swept away by the torrents of events that continually flow past us in all directions, rocking and shocking us.

For instance, since the secret launching of Operation Champagne last January, a large number of young French conscripts in Algeria have been taught (more or less against their will) how to torture fellaghas, and people suspected of being or hiding fellaghas, and people suspected of knowing something about the possible hiding places of potential fellaghas — in other words, pretty much anyone and everyone in the native population. . . . Meanwhile, the Federal Republic of Germany is on its way to becoming the most affluent country in Europe. . . . Mao Ze-dong, even as he appreciatively takes in the fragrance of his Hundred Flowers, is warming up for the Great Leap Forward. . . . Russia has sent *Sputnik 1* into orbit, inaugurating a brand new planetary era. . . . And the American president — yes, the selfsame Dwight Eisenhower whose armed forces crushed the Wehrmacht in 1945, is starting to cast sidelong glances at a little country called Vietnam.

The Lepages of the Rue de Seine are not particularly well-informed on these matters. Although Raphael buys *Le Monde* every day, just as his father used to buy *Le Temps,* he rarely does more than riffle through its pages, glancing distractedly at the headlines. And Saffie, to say the least, is not a fanatic follower of current events. Both of them, albeit for different reasons, carry on their existence at a remove from that particular level of reality. Saffie's mind is hermetically sealed around her pain, like an oyster around its pearl. And Raphael — his brain wholly taken up with the effort of thinking simultaneously about his pregnant wife and his evening concert — is better endowed with concentration than with curiosity.

Thus, when they wake up on the morning of October 17 to discover that neither the light switches nor the gas stove nor the streetlamps are working, and when they hear the din of a monstrous traffic jam coming from the Odéon intersection a hundred and fifty yards away, they haven't a clue as to what is going on. They haven't been following the power company's crescendo of complaints and threats over the past few weeks. And when the Nobel committee, later that same day, decides to award its prize in literature to Albert Camus, they're oblivious to the political implications of this choice. They know nothing about Camus, haven't read a line of his books, aren't even aware that he's a pied noir — a Frenchman born in Algeria.

Saffie's pregnancy is going badly; that's what's on their minds.

For the first four months, she loses rather than gains weight. Eats next to nothing. What food she does manage to get down, with Raphael's patient encouragement, she immediately brings up again. Deprived of nourishment, the child starts feeding on its mother's bones. Saffie's already lackluster beauty vanishes altogether — the flesh melts away from her face, revealing the outlines of her skull; the circles under her eyes deepen and darken; her gums bleed; her strength deserts her.

She no longer goes food shopping on the Rue de Buci. In fact, she ceases cooking entirely, for the mere sight of meat makes her stomach heave. Raphael is forced to fall back on his young bachelor's habits, eating most of his meals alone, either at home or in one of the neighborhood cafes.

On the other hand, Saffie continues to keep up with her housekeeping duties — in fact it's exhausting just to watch her work. Maria-Felice was capable of leaving Raphael's old slippers lying where they were, splayed at the foot of his favorite armchair, so that he'd find them there when he looked for them the next day. Saffie puts everything away at once. Sometimes she puts things away so well he needs her help to find them.

Dismayed, he questions Martin — had Michelle behaved as oddly as this during her pregnancies? No . . . not that he could remember . . . not in the same way, anyhow.

When he comes home in the evening, the sight of Saffie sitting motionless at the kitchen table in the dark (even on days without power strikes), makes him quake with fear.

$$\cdot \qquad \cdot \qquad \cdot \qquad \cdot \qquad \cdot$$

The worst of it, and by far, is that she no longer wants to share his bed. On the pretext that her insomnia prevents him from getting a good night's sleep and that he needs to be in shape to play the flute, she's taken to sleeping on a foldout couch in the study at the other end of the apartment. Raphael shakes his head in disbelief — after three months of marriage, they're already sleeping apart?

One morning, he comes into the study when Saffie happens to be in the bathroom, and sees something protruding from under her sheets. Walks across the room and picks it up. Turns it over, staring at it in puzzlement. Just then Saffie reenters the room — and, leaping at him in a fury, snatches the stuffed poodle paw from his hands.

"Give me that!"

A cry of despair. Raphael is stunned. He makes no move to resist.

"Saffie, what is it?" he asks her in a low voice.

"It's mine!" screams Saffie, shaking. And then, embarrassed at the intensity of her own reaction, she adds, "It's nothing. A toy . . . when I was a little girl. That's why . . . I'm sorry. . . ."

"But what *is* it?"

"It's silly. You would mock me. . . ."

"Come on, Saffie. . . . Have I ever made fun of you?"

Stuffing the object back under her pillow, Saffie makes her bed at top speed, as impeccably as a nurse or a soldier.

"Come on. I make you some coffee?"

.   .   .   .   .   .

This is perhaps the longest conversation they have all fall.

Yes. They're speaking to each other less and less. Saffie's enigmatic silence may have been one of the reasons Raphael fell in love with her — but now that she's his wife, and particularly now that she's carrying his child, it's not the same. Her silences are heavy and ominous. *Why* is she behaving like this? As he can't bear the sensation of anxiety, he finds it hard even to think about it.

In a sense, until he married Saffie, Raphael never knew what a problem was. His father's death had saddened him, naturally, but it wasn't exactly what you could call a problem.

He has no idea how to deal with adversity.

When Martin and Michelle call to ask how his wife is getting on, he keeps his answers vague and optimistic. "You can see it now!" he says, for instance.

Yes, you can see it now. A pitiful little ball. Like the offspring of the larger ball Saffie turned into that day last summer, when Raphael set the alarm clock without warning her. Aghast, he realizes that by contrast with their present mute tension, that morning of screaming and confusion has virtually become a memory of happiness.

"I'm sure everything will turn out all right," he tells Michelle another day, on the telephone. "But she . . . well, she does seem a bit despondent now and then."

"Maybe she has some secret sorrow?" suggests Michelle. "Maybe she saw a baby die in the war or something, and her pregnancy is dredging up bad memories. You never know. . . . Does she cry often?"

Raphael is brought up short.

"No," he says after a long silence, running his fingers again and again through his nonexistent hair. "Come to think of it, I've never seen her cry. Not once."

He's counting on the child's arrival in the month of March to smooth things out, lighten the atmosphere between them. . . . Yes, he's absolutely counting on it. It's clear that for some unknown reason, Saffie's terrified of having this baby. But when it actually arrives, it'll be real — it'll be *this* little boy and not another. . . . And who ever heard of a mother who didn't find her own son irresistible?

From then on, things will surely get better. *They have to.*

In the meantime, though, Saffie's misery seeps through the cracks beneath the doors, infecting every square inch of the Rue de Seine apartment, poisoning the very air. How can Raphael be expected to breathe this vitiated air into his precious solid silver Louis Lot? For Jolivet's *Five Incantations,* the piece he's working on now, he needs the full strength of his art.

He begins to practice even his solos at the orchestra's offices near Porte d'Orléans, getting home late almost every night.

(Other women? No. The idea doesn't even cross his mind. He's in love with Saffie. Moved by her pregnancy. And helpless in the face of her misery.)

The days drag by. They're the shortest days of the year, but they drag by. The long nights drag by, too.

One evening, after an exceptionally trying meal (on the menu — prepared by and for Raphael because Saffie can't bear the odor of cooking fat: fried eggs and fried potatoes, the latter unfortunately cooked over too high a flame for too short a time so that they ended up burned on the outside, raw on the inside, and all but inedible; for Saffie: butterless crackers and sugarless tea), the phone rings.

Raphael picks up the receiver.

"Mama!"

He can't help it. His little boy's heart leaps with joy.

"Well!" says Hortense Trala-Lepage. And adds, after a short silence — "How are you?"

"Fine, fine," murmurs Raphael, paralyzed.

Even if Saffie weren't with him in the dining room, he'd find it hard to open up to his mother about his situation. A brief summary of his life after six months of marriage to the German maid? "Fine, fine . . ."

"You'll be coming down for Christmas, of course?" Hortense goes on. There's an unprecedented note of courtesy, almost of shyness, in her voice. Raphael can tell she's terrified he might say no.

"For Christmas?" he repeats stupidly, to gain time.

Never in their lives have the Lepage mother and son been separated at Christmas. A series of school Nativities goes flashing through the son's mind — both his parents in the audience, staring worshipfully at their corkscrew-curled child rigged out in shepherd's garb as he played melodies on Pan's flute in a corner of the stage. . . . Every year without fail, his mother's cheeks would be glistening with tears when he joined them after the performance. . . . Why doesn't Saffie ever cry? . . .

The silence is getting awkward and Raphael knows he has to come up with an answer. Any answer, but fast.

"Er, well . . . Oh, Mother, it'd be so nice if we could come down —"

"I'm not inviting both of you." (Though she's interrupting him, his mother is careful to keep a bit of treacle in her voice.) "I'm inviting *you.* Oh, Raphael, don't tell me you're going to make me celebrate Christmas alone with Maria-Felice!?"

"Mother!" says Raphael, quite overcome. And, lowering his voice so that Saffie won't hear him — but Saffie's already in the kitchen, washing up with frightening efficiency — he adds, "I'm a married man now! You're going to have to accept that sooner or later!"

"I'm sorry," says Hortense, in a voice that does, in fact, sound sorry. "I simply *cannot* meet that woman."

"Mother . . . *That woman,* as you call her, happens to be carrying your grandson in her womb."

A lengthy silence ensues at the other end of the line. At last a series of stifled sobs reaches Raphael's ears.

"My little Mammoth — please don't cry, I beg of you, you're breaking my heart."

"You're breaking *mine!"*

"Mother, please! Please calm down. . . . I miss you, you know that? I miss the house, too. . . . What's the weather like down there? And how is dear old Maria-Felice?"

"Next year," says his mother, "or whenever you like, you can come down for a visit with the little one. *He's* innocent. But as far as she's concerned . . . no, I can't bring myself . . . after all we went through . . ."

Thus it is that Raphael and Saffie spend their first Christmas on the Rue de Seine alone together.

It's not easy, though, to celebrate Christmas with someone who refuses to eat.

With a heavy heart, Raphael goes down to the local caterer's and orders a meal for himself. He sets the table — fine white tablecloth, gold-embroidered white napkins, silver cutlery and candlesticks, flute glasses. With considerable difficulty, he convinces Saffie to take a sip of Veuve Clicquot.

"To your health, my darling . . . and to the health of our child."

She makes no answer.

"I love you, Saffie."

"I love you, too."

But she doesn't say his name. (Has she ever said it? He can't recall.)

Every time they stop talking, silence looms between them, gray and heavy as a cement wall.

"Next year we'll get a Christmas tree, right?" says Raphael with false gaiety. "For our baby. There's no point in having one this year, just for the two of us."

She says nothing.

"Did you have a Christmas tree at home, when you were little?"

Driven to despair by his wife's silence, Raphael launches into the only song he knows in German (he has a lovely singing voice):

"O Tannenbaum, o Tannenbaum . . ."

"Stop it!" says Saffie sharply, glowering at him.

Raphael lowers his head. Goes back to eating his turkey with chestnut stuffing.

"But tell me . . . ," he can't help adding ten minutes later, determined to dispel at all costs the silence that's making a mockery of their festive table, "did your parents take you to church at Christmas?"

"Yes, of course," says Saffie conciliatingly.

"My father was an atheist, he refused to even set foot in a church, but my mother insisted I go as far as First Communion. And then she and I would attend Mass together, at least every Christmas and Easter. . . . I used to love singing Christmas carols! You know — if you like — we could go to midnight Mass at Notre Dame after dinner. It'd be beautiful. . . . All the carols . . . Even if you don't know the words, the melodies will probably be the same. . . ."

"No, not tonight. I'm tired."

"*Not tonight?*" says Raphael in exasperation. "But tomorrow it won't be Christmas Eve! Oh . . . do as you like."

The silence returns at once — and at once he feels the need to break it.

"Did . . . did you stop believing in God one day, too?"

Saffie's green eyes throw out flames at him, telling him: *You're breaking the rules, coming too close.*

But who wrote the damned rules in the first place? wonders Raphael. He resolves to stand up to her for a change, counter her, shake her up a bit — he wants to hear her pronounce at least one sentence that comes directly from the heart. She's given him her body the way you throw a bone to the dog, never sharing anything truly intimate with him — her past, the music of her soul . . .

"What did your father do? Before the war, I mean."

To his surprise, Saffie answers simply, "A doctor for animals."

"Veterinarian?"

"Yes. Vet-er-in-arian," she articulates.

"And your mother?"

"And my mother . . . ," says Saffie, inexplicably turning purple. "My mother, she was a mother."

And she rises to clear the table.

We can never sit around just drinking and talking until two in the morning, thinks Raphael. Whereas that's one of the things I love doing most in the whole world. Dear Lord . . . will I ever be able to do it again?

"I go to bed," announces Saffie, the minute she's finished with the dishes.

And that is the end of their Christmas dinner.

Raphael plays the flute.

His playing is getting better by the day, as anguish has come to lend added complexity to his ingenuous, overly optimistic nature — enhancing rather than supplanting his mad love, slipping into the interstices of his music and giving it new shades, denser and more subtle shades than ever before. In the adagio movements in particular, every note he produces is like the shimmering surface of a pond beneath which dark treasures lurk.

All the members of the orchestra are struck by it — Lepage is playing like a man possessed — as if his life depended on it. He's turning into one of the important flutists of his generation. Rampal hears him, and takes note.

And Saffie . . . well, Saffie does the housework. Unrelentingly.

One icy day toward the end of January, she's scrubbing the kitchen floor with bleach as she does every Monday, Wednesday, and Friday morning, when a dull pain stealthily creeps up on her, crushes her innards and retreats, fading into nothingness.

"Raphael!" she cries out in panic, when she recovers the use of speech.

They're in the ambulance, in the driving rain.

"It's far too early," mutters Raphael in a tense, low voice. "Six weeks is far too much. Hopefully they'll give you something to stop the contractions . . . and then you should take it easy, you should probably stay in bed. . . . Oh, Saffie! Did you really have to wash the kitchen floor? No one ever goes into the kitchen anyway, the floor isn't even dirty!"

He's sick with fear at the thought they might lose the child. Sweat runs down his forehead like the rain down the windshield. Saffie isn't listening to him. She doesn't even know who he is. Mute and terror-stricken, she clutches onto him blindly and sinks her teeth into his raw silk scarf every two or three minutes, to keep from crying out.

The ambulance sets them down outside the maternity ward of a large hospital (not the one she was taken to for her aborted abortion), and Raphael watches as his wife, her face twisted, unrecognizable, is rolled away to the sacred martyrdom of mothers.

Dear God . . . , he says to himself. Dear God, please . . .

In 1958, men don't accompany their wives into the labor room. They don't attend, cowed and helpless, the crucifixion of the body they love. When their offspring is ejected from its infernal paradise, still dripping with blood and glair, they're not there to grasp it, half-nauseous and half-ecstatic, head awhirl. . . . No, in 1958 they have the right to remain peacefully apart from all of this in the waiting room, as clean and dry as the thinking beings for which they take themselves. Proverbially, they pass the time by pacing the room and chain-smoking. Since Raphael, unlike the four or five other near-fathers in the waiting room, doesn't smoke, he has to be content with running his left hand repeatedly over his balding pate. For once, his double concentration has deserted him — were he to pick up one of the old issues of *Paris-Match* lying on the table, he'd be utterly incapable of following a news story. His whole being is strained toward the event that's taking place at this very moment, so close to him and yet out of his sight — the birth or death, he doesn't know which, of his first child. . . .

Why in heaven's name did she have to scrub that floor?

The cries of the other parturients can be heard through the closed doors. Sometimes he can make out actual words *("He-e-e-elp!" "I'm gonna di-i-i-i-i-e!" "No-o-o-o-o-o-o!" "Jesus Chri-i-i-*

ist!"), but mostly what reaches his ears are heartrending sobs, inarticulate moans and savage screeches . . . enough to make you give up flirting once and for all.

Good Lord! sighs Raphael, shaken. He tries to imagine Hortense screaming this way as she struggled to push him out from between her thighs . . . and rapidly puts an end to the attempt.

Listen as he may, he can't distinguish Saffie's scream among the others . . . but then, would he recognize her scream if he heard it? It wouldn't necessarily be the same scream as the one he heard last summer, so weirdly high-pitched and childlike. . . .

The fact is that Saffie isn't screaming at all. Not because she's more stoical than the other soon-to-be-mothers, but because, ten minutes ago, she was given a general anesthesia. Now her face and legs are concealed by a sheet and the obstetrician is in the process of slitting her stomach open with a scalpel.

Couldn't give birth, poor thing.

Didn't want to push.

Nothing for it now, though — like it or not, she'll have the child.

Ah! You see? There he is — already curled up in the doctor's hands! A boy. Not pretty. Blue. A runty blue boy baby.

They carry him off — fast, faster! — he needs oxygen, perfusions, transfusions — but his heart is beating — yes — boom *boom*, boom *boom* — yes, he's alive!

He weighs less than four pounds. That's low, even for a seven-and-a-half-month-old fetus.

His mother didn't want to feed him.

Gave him nothing but her bones to eat.

Now Saffie's lying there, annihilated, gut agape, surrounded by anesthesiologists and nurses. She's bleeding, she's already lost a lot of blood but no one's paying attention to her, everyone is rushing around madly to save the child, indeed the obstetrician has already left the room but now he's running back, here he comes, in a dither, he's quite young, only recently completed his internship, finds this crisis unnerving but wants to prove he can take it in his stride — and so, faced with the necessity of curbing the hemorrhage at all costs, the decision he makes is clear-cut —

"Out it comes."

The nurses are shocked, so are the anesthesiologists, but it's up to the doctor to decide — so, calmly, he proceeds to ablate the organ in question, then sew the unconscious woman up again, layer by layer, stapling and stitching. . . . Her abdomen will be permanently defaced by a long and ugly purple scar.

Raphael's alone now in the waiting room, and his solitude only serves to exacerbate his fear. If he had hair on the top of his head, he'd be tearing it out by the handful. He's standing still, eyes pressed tightly shut, clutching his head with both hands. It so happens that all the other men have gone to join their spent spouses and their bawling babes, and that Raphael is the only one who hasn't been called. He's gagging with fear. Touchingly (for he embraced his father's dispassionate atheism years ago), he's praying. Old prayers from his catechism days have welled up in his throat, and he's reciting them one after the other in a low voice, like rosary beads, *Hail Mary full of grace, Our Father who art in heaven, The Lord is my shepherd, I shall not want.* . . . Having rummaged through his memory and come up with nothing else, he begins again, *Hail Mary full of grace* . . .

"Monsieur Lepage?"

The nurse's voice is far too amiable. His child must be dead.

"Would you like to see your son?"

A shower of felicity. Undescribable joy floods through him, and relief, leaving him speechless.

Let's go with him now, and take a look at this tiny person in its incubator. What do you mean, you don't like babies? Oh, come on now, come along anyway — on tiptoe, shhh! — you'll see. This is no ordinary baby, I promise you. The chubby pink slobberers whose strollers crowd our city parks are just as repulsive to me as they are to you. But this baby . . . no, seriously, this one's different. He's . . . I'm not sure how to put it. . . . Even though he's no bigger than your two fists stacked on top of each other . . . he's already *someone*. Look how rapidly he's breathing. Look at the black tufts of hair sticking up every which way from his damp head. Look at his emaciated little face, with its astonishingly expressive surfaces and angles. Look at the green glints coming from his dark eyes through the half-open slits of his eyelids. At the age of only thirty minutes, this little boy already radiates an exceptional sensitivity.

Raphael doesn't have the right to take him in his arms, or even to touch him. The child is under glass for the time being. They've just barely managed to save him from limbo. But now — no doubt about it — Emil is going to live.

Raphael's cheeks are bathed in tears.

And Saffie? Saffie . . . Still out cold.

VII

A month has gone by.

Saffie came home from hospital first — and then, a fortnight later, weighing a full five pounds, Emil. (At the registry office, Raphael spelled his son's name with an *e* at the end so it would look French, but in Saffie's mind it's spelled German-style, without the *e*. And we shall soon be spending some time in Saffie's mind.)

She has no milk. Of course. What little she did have dried up during the two weeks of their separation, while Emil was being cared for in the incubator and Raphael went to the hospital every day, without Saffie, to visit him. The pediatric nurses, having foreseen before the young woman's discharge that her milk would dry up, had shown her how to sterilize baby bottles and prepare the child's "formula" — measuring milk powder, adding mineral water (flat, not sparkling!), heating the mixture to exactly body temperature (no higher or you'll burn his throat! no lower or you'll give him convulsions!). They'd also shown her how to bathe the child (without drowning it!) and how to change its diapers (without jabbing safety pins into its stomach!). . . .

Raphael does his best to convince himself that their happily married life will finally be able to get under way, now that the child is out of danger, now that it's truly come to live with them upon the earth. He goes to a nearby printer's, orders fancy birth announcements (midnight blue paper with gold lettering), and sends out dozens of them — to his mother, his friends, the other members of the orchestra. . . .

Saffie sends out not a single one.

Raphael calls his friends in Clichy to let them know that mother and child are doing fine. Soon, he promises, they'll be able to come over and meet the future owner of the Trala vineyards, Burgundian as well as Algerian. But the days go by, and he doesn't invite them over. For the time being, Saffie is still acting too strangely.

She's started cleaning house again. Somewhat less than she had during her pregnancy — but still far more than necessary. She doesn't know how to spend time with her child, who's turning out to be almost as apathetic as she is. Emil sleeps little, calls for his mother rarely, almost never cries. But he doesn't gurgle, either. It can't be normal, thinks Raphael, for a newborn baby to be so quiet and serious. When he sees Emil in his basket, lying calmly on his back, eyes wide open, limbs inert, while his mother darts about the room armed with a can of furniture spray and a dustcloth, it makes shivers go down his spine.

She doesn't know how to hold the child. After bathing it, she dries it in a terrycloth towel and then just stands there, stiffly and uncertainly, holding the twitching naked baby almost vertically. Or else she sits down with it in a chair next to the window, with the freezing February air eddying against the windowpanes — and it's as if the child doesn't exist for her. She just sits there, not looking at him, staring into the void, until Emil begins to whimper with hunger or cold.

"Would you like me to hire someone?" asks Raphael gently. "To help you? . . ."

"Help me?" says Saffie. "I don't need help."

More distant, more inaccessible than ever.

Seeing his wife so awkward and distracted in looking after the child, Raphael has a faint premonition of despair. Oh, nothing like the immense, irremediable despair that will engulf him a few years from now. Just a premonition of it.

For the time being, in spite of everything, he's too enchanted by his discovery of fatherhood to be miserable. The minute he gets home from a rehearsal or a concert, he slips into Emil's room to make sure he's still there, still alive and breathing. Soon, the child recognizes its father's step, quivers at the smell of his body, responds to his arrival in the room by kicking up its legs and letting out little yelps of pleasure. Raphael never tires of gazing at his son — a bit on the scrawny side, to be sure, but still, unutterably beautiful with his glowing black ember eyes, his slender branch limbs, his tiny twig fingers, and his head which, at the age of one month, is already covered with a soft black down that's starting to wave . . . ah, yes! he'll have his father's lovely curls.

What an impenetrable mystery, says Raphael to himself. A mixture of the two of us. Myself, plus Saffie, plus a touch of miracle, add up to . . . you.

Sometimes, leaning over his son's crib, his eyes fill with tears. Taking Emil's incredibly small hands in his own, he strokes the wrinkled fingers curled on his giant palm, presses them to his lips, and murmurs, "A musician's hands . . . You'll be gifted, my boy. No doubt about it."

Toward the middle of February, Raphael goes back into his music room for the first time in months, and once again Saffie hears sweet flute trills come lilting toward her across the apartment. Her husband's lips purse and tighten, pucker and relax, sculpting the column of air that splits into two as it passes over the opening in the mouthpiece. His tongue expertly articulates the musical phrases, detaching the notes from one another, attacking staccatos like a little dagger, *takatak, takatakata*.

It's with these same lips and tongue that . . . but, almost invariably, Saffie turns away when her husband tries to kiss her. She dislikes the sensation of Raphael's avid lips pressed hard against hers, his pointy tongue seeking out hers.

Early in March, Raphael has to go to Milan for a series of concerts. He won't be away long — only three days — but he does have to go.

"Will you be all right?" he asks Saffie, his eyes reiterating the question.

"Of course."

"Here's the phone number of my hotel. . . . If anything comes up, if there's any problem whatsoever, you can always call on

Mademoiselle Blanche. Okay? She's very kind. . . . Are you sure you'll be all right?"

Saffie nods.

    ·   ·   ·   ·   ·   ·   ·

It's Raphael's first day away.

The child is there. She's set it down on the living-room rug. Emil gets cold and starts to cry — softly, tearlessly. Saffie finishes dusting the living-room furniture. Then she picks the baby up and lays it in its crib.

"Go to sleep," she tells it.

In the adjacent bathroom, she takes a load of Emil's diapers from the washing machine, begins to hang them up . . . and gets lost.

It happens because the day is sunny and springlike, and because disposable diapers haven't been invented yet. As she's hanging up the white rectangles of cotton, a ray of sunlight falls on one of them and she plummets into a blur of whiteness, blinding sunlight glancing off white sheets and pillow slips . . .

She's helping her mother hang up the washing outdoors, in the garden behind their house, it's springtime — no, not that springtime, not that one, a springtime before the fear, '42 perhaps, or '43 — yes, she can only be five or six because the clothesline is very high and to reach it she has to stand on tiptoe. . . .

What fun they had that day! The wind kept tearing the sheets out of their hands before they could pin them to the clothesline, and they'd run to pick them up on the lawn, laughing uncontrollably (oh what a green! what a white! the white of sheets back then, and the green of grass — perfect colors, paradigms, lost forever), then hang them up again, all the while singing together in harmony, *Kommt ein Vogel geflogen,* Saffie's mother singing the soprano and Saffie, whose voice was deeper, the alto, a little bird flew up to me with a letter in its beak, a letter *von der Mutter,* from my mother; as it turned out Saffie never did receive a letter from her mother; as it turned out her mother found a different way to use sheets — but what fun they'd had that day! Dancing, laughing, playing hide-and-seek among the wind-whipped laundry . . . Mutti! When Emil starts to talk, he'll call her not Mutti but Maman. Mutti is over and done with and so is Muttersprache, both have been suspended, once and for all. . . .

She's finished hanging up the diapers. Panting, her heart thumping, a dreadful weight pressing on her chest, she goes down the hallway to Emil's room and takes him from his crib. He's not crying yet, but it's time for his midmorning meal. Hugging him to her, she rocks and rocks him — not crazily! not violently! — and he nuzzles hungrily against her empty breasts, still not crying.

Tiny thing.

Carrying him to the kitchen, she sets him down on the table while she goes about preparing his formula — yes, just like that, plumps him down like a package (he hasn't learned to roll over yet, so he can't fall off the table onto the floor — but still, it's unsettling to see a human treated so nonchalantly). When his bottle is ready, she picks him up again and slides the rubber nipple between his lips. Emil's dark eyes devour his mother's face as he drinks and his own face comes to life; his tiny nostrils pump air and his eyebrows work up and down, making him look surprised and anxious in rapid alternation. . . .

Momentarily, he drifts off to sleep. Saffie studies his translucent eyelids in fascination — they're like microscopic landmaps, with the blue veins as rivers. His eyelashes flutter — what fugitive scene has just flashed through his mind? What can a newborn baby have to dream about? He awakens with a faint sigh, tightens his lips around the nipple . . .

Saffie is scared.

Shaking herself, she lays Emil against her shoulder (as she was taught to do at the hospital), pats him on the back, waits for his burp, then lowers him back into the curve of her arm. She's amazed at how totally her son trusts her, surrendering himself to her embrace, not even suspecting that by squeezing him more tightly, a little more tightly . . .

It's appallingly easy.

She knows this thanks to Monsieur Ferrat or rather Julien, her high school French teacher in Tegel who, after classes had let out in the summer of '52, when she was fifteen years old and he thirty-two, had decided that she should become his friend, and then somewhat more than his friend — his hostage, if you like — and who, having once decided this, had felt the need to enlighten her in every way — to emancipate her, as it were, body and mind. Saffie hadn't deemed it necessary to disabuse her teacher on the subject of her physical innocence (she'd been deflowered years before); on the other hand, where the genocide of the Jews was concerned, her virginity was intact. All she had was a faint memory of the posters that had cropped up on the rare walls still standing in their neighborhood in the summer of '45 — posters on which the photograph (mountains of naked corpses) had been as impenetrable to her as the legend *("This is your fault!")*.

Julien Ferrat was aware that this topic was never broached in Saffie's entourage, either at home or at school, but he felt capable of supervising her education in the matter because, as a student and movie buff in Lyons immediately after the war, he'd sat through innumerable horrifying newsreels of the camp liberations and Nuremberg trials — proofs of German guilt that were shown ad nauseam to the French, to reassure them as to their own innocence. Thus, in the macabre history class he administered to Saffie throughout the summer, Monsieur Ferrat or rather Julien made it a point of honor to be as thorough as possible; the nubile girl learned all there was to know about Krystallnacht, elderly Jewish men forced to lower their trousers in the street (until then she'd never so much as heard the word circumcision), gold teeth yanked out of corpses, soap made from human fat and lampshades from human skin. . . .

. . . And then, about that too.

It's appallingly easy, the young teacher on vacation had explained to his stunned student, all the while stroking her nascent breasts: it's so tiny, like a baby cat, a baby rabbit, it's nothing at all, you just grab its feet the way the doctor does at birth, both feet fit easily into the circle between your thumb and index finger, you dangle the child head downward, swing it back and forth a couple of times and there you go! — it's done, the skull is soft, it's so easy, the mother is screaming, the tiny head is smashed, all that's left of it are little splashes of brain and blood, the tiny person is over, done with — Aus, vorbei — laughing, you toss it on the ground and move on to the next one.

Saffie is holding Emil in her arms. She stares at him — sleeping now, his short black curls sticking to his head with sweat. Though he's fast asleep, she can see the green-black crescent of his pupils through the narrow slit between his eyelids.

Her own eyes close.

She watches a Nazi man performing the gesture — seizing the baby's ankles in the circle between his thumb and index finger, swinging it back and forth to gather momentum, then smashing the little body against a brick wall or the side of a truck or a cement floor — and she holds the image — stop, photo, freeze. . . . Moving in closer, she examines the Nazi's fine young body, his slim strong muscular limbs — yes, this too is a body, no more no less, this body, too, once suckled its mother's breasts, she's unable to keep her gaze trained on the man's face, his marble blue eyes, his steel-trap jaws, his sarcastically grinning lips — but his body, yes, let's take his body, it's suspended outside of time and Saffie, gliding toward him with her eyes closed, gently removes his shiny black boots, then the trousers and jacket of his uniform — and gradually, as she undresses it, the Nazi's body relaxes, softens and shrinks . . . turning at last into little Emil, sound asleep in his mother Saffie's arms.

She presses her baby to her chest, feels like throwing up, studies the thin crack of its eyes through the eyelashes, inhales the fragrance of its skin, listens to the faint gust of its breath — and also, from outside, the twittering of the birds of Paris, nothing but pigeons and sparrows in this season, early March — *Raphael, please come home! Why did you have to leave?*

Vati isn't home, he's gone away somewhere, like all the other fathers, it's a strange world with no men around, the only men left in the village are the elderly and the simpleminded, the ill and the insane, you can't count the Fremdarbeiter who've come to work in the fields, they're not real men but rather enemy prisoners, the real men are far away fighting the enemy, the whole world is our enemy, the enemy surrounds us, they want to kill us so the men have to protect us, they send us letters, the women spend their time reading the men's letters out loud, over and over again, but the men almost never come home, only once a year on leave, or else dead in uniform, like Herr Silber the man next door, but not Vati — no, Vati doesn't wear a uniform and he isn't going to die because he's deaf in one ear, lucky for him, he gets to work in Leverkusen, it's an important job — in a laboratory, like a magician — looking for remedies, not for animals this time but for human beings, to help them sleep. . . .

It's the second day of Raphael's absence and Saffie's in the living room, huddled in a corner of the leather couch, rocking Emil. Everything is calm, the pigeons are cooing and the sparrows are chirping but apart from that everything is calm, the wooden furniture gleams and day follows night, Saffie hasn't slept a wink for the past two nights, she's frightened and everything is calm.

That's what is so incredible, every time it happens all is calm and peaceful, it's a lovely day, music and the smells of Sunday cooking are floating through the open windows, people are out in their backyards, tinkering with bicycles or gossiping, and then suddenly all hell breaks loose — screams, rubble, mutilated corpses — then all is calm again, the silence returns, the blue sky smiles serenely. . . .

Saffie is rocking Emil in her arms, he's six weeks old, he's had his bottle, burped, and drifted off to sleep, now a smile wafts across his face and milk dribbles from one corner of his mouth. She wipes it off with the edge of his bib.

Men's smells are absent from every household, there isn't the least whiff of leather or tobacco or male sweat, the houses smell of nettle soup and maternal fear, on feast days the old men of the village play Strauss waltzes as best they can . . . and the women dance with other women.

Saffie's mother is singing. She's rocking two-month-old Peter in her arms, the child of last year's leave — yes, because the job at Bayer's isn't a sinecure, it's still military service, Vati can't travel when and where he likes — Peter has buried his little head between his mother's breasts and she's singing very softly, to him and to all of them, *Alle meine Entchen schwimmen auf dem See,* all my little ducklings swimming in the lake, swimming in the lake, there are five of them clustered around her, their fifty fingers grasping to touch her, any part of her, a lock of hair, a patch of arm, a fold of dress, anything, *Köpfchen in das Wasser, Schwänzchen in die Höh. . . .* She goes on singing and rocking Peter in her arms and it's almost impossible to hear anything else, almost impossible, their heads in the water, their tails in the air, no, the humming vibration you feel in Mutti's flesh comes from her song, not from the bombers, but then there's no denying it any longer, what they hear behind the song is indeed the familiar drone — and then — here it comes — a long whistle and the night sky explodes into fireworks, a million-candled Tannenbaum, and Saffie isn't there anymore, she's nothing but pure clean icy panic, upheaval and overthrow, a dizzying rush of air, the detonations seem to be taking place inside her own head, cracking and fissuring the plated bone structure of her skull — then comes the high-pitched tinkle of glass as it shatters and scatters — ha ha ha ha ha! witch laughter! carnival! — and then — a scream.

A long, an endless woman's scream that seems to split your head in two the way lightning splits the sky. Coming not from our house — no, all of us are still here, still huddled together in a corner of the room, a trembling mountain of limbs — no, from next door. The Silbers' house must have been hit this time, will that scream never cease? How can it just go on and on like that?

Finally, it's over. The planes have withdrawn and silence has returned, except for the sobbing of Frau Silber. It's her turn today, not ours, her roof has fallen in and her daughter Lotte, seven-and-a-half-years old — Saffie's best friend Lotte, with whom she plays board games on Sunday afternoons, *Mensch, ärgere dich nicht* is their favorite, don't lose your temper, that's the name of the game, that's life, if I land on the same space as you it's just too bad, you'll have to go back to the beginning and wait until you throw a six before you can come out again, you throw the die over and over but you never get a six, that's just too bad, there's no point in losing your temper, you have to learn to be a good sport, that's what the game is about, that's what life's about, education, good manners, life will always have its ups and downs so you might as well get used to it now, you can heave a sigh if you like but then it's best just to shrug your shoulders and laugh it off, because those are the rules of the game, you see? — is pinned beneath the roofbeam, her right arm and leg reduced to mush.

Saffie rushes next door with her mother. Lotte is still lying there, inert, unconscious — dead? — no, not dead, breathing, but with her arm and leg crushed by the oaken beam, a mess of mushed flesh.

Emil is fast asleep. *Siren!* Fear clogs Saffie's throat. Before she's had time to think, before her brain can undertake the least reasoning in her defense (peacetime not wartime, Paris not Berlin, adult not child), she chokes.

Doorbell not siren.

You go to the door, you open it and nothing explodes, no one is dead.

It's the concierge, Mademoiselle Blanche. She apologizes, saying she hopes Saffie won't think she's interfering, but . . . well, she hasn't seen anyone come out of Monsieur Lepage's apartment since his departure forty-eight hours ago, and she was beginning to get a bit worried. She thought maybe she should stop by and make sure everything was all right.

"Here, Madame," she says, holding out a large but perfectly flat envelope. "It wouldn't fit under the door."

Her lie makes her puffy speckled face turn crimson, darkening even the moles a shade — but this doesn't prevent her from taking a close look at the young woman. Yes, Madame Lapage does seem a bit distraught. . . . Even thinner and paler than usual, if that's possible. . . . But apart from that, there's nothing untoward in her appearance — her clothes and hair are as nondescript and as impeccable as ever.

"The baby's sleeping," Saffie tells Mademoiselle Blanche, as if to justify the child's absence from her field of vision. She's on the point of adding, "He's alive," but the concierge is already backing off, a finger on her lips.

"Oh, I'm sorry! He's having his morning nap! I hope the doorbell didn't wake him!"

And she vanishes. Her mind now at rest. How kind of her, truly.

Saffie's memory almost stops there. She can't remember what happened next, whether the neighborhood women and their swarms of kids managed to move the roofbeam by themselves without causing the rest of the house to collapse, or whether outside help eventually arrived — ambulances, cranes, firetrucks. . . . Her memory almost stops there, but there's one last image — the image of lilacs — yes, lilacs swaying in the wind — because it was a windy April day and growing in front of Frau Silber's house were lilac bushes of all three colors, white, mauve, violet, the wind was a delight to breathe in and the fragrance of the lilacs made Saffie's nostrils tickle — no one had hurt the lilacs, you see, they were as graceful and carefree as if the world had just been created, as if God had just glanced approvingly at his creation before going off to bed — averting his gaze from the house in which Lotte, pinned beneath the roofbeam, had fainted away in pain, *Mensch, ärgere dich nicht,* no point in losing your temper, it's just a game, all you can do is laugh and start all over again — and if you lose, well, you'd better laugh anyway because the most important thing is to prove you're a good sport. . . .

Saffie puts Emil down in his room, the room of a little French boy, with airplane-patterned wallpaper, stuffed toys lined up on the shelves, a neatly ordered chest of drawers (pajamas in the top drawer, undershirts in the middle, and rompers in the bottom), a crib — and, next to the crib, a changing table with a bottle of mineral water, skin lotion, talcum powder for diaper rash, a tiny little comb and a tiny little brush with silky bristles for the baby's silky hair. . . .

After covering him with his quilt (just the body, not the head!), she winds up his music box, a present from his paternal grandmother, which plays the theme song from Tchaikovsky's *Swan Lake.*

Musical instruments are as asinine as birds, thinks Saffie. They don't know how to shut up. Lilacs will never stop swaying in the wind, the wind will never stop blowing, the sky will never stop smiling serenely, and birds and flutes will never stop singing. . . .

Lotte is dead. They couldn't manage to move the roofbeam or to bring in outside help, she's still lying there and now she's dead, dead — and since she was her mother's only child, Frau Silber is sitting on the doorstep with her forehead on her knees and her arms around her legs, rocking back and forth, gently, ceaselessly, like the lilacs. When dusk falls, Saffie's mother comes out and gently takes the arm of Lotte's — now no one's — mother, and leads her over to their house, which, this day, is still standing. She's made milk-and-potato soup but no one's mother isn't hungry; going over to a corner of the room, next to the cold woodstove, she sits down in the same position, forehead on knees, arms around legs, and resumes her rocking. . . .

Saffie and her brothers, sisters, mother, in a circle around the table, join their palms, lower their heads, and fervently thank God for all the blessings he's showered upon them. Life is sheer bliss for all of them that evening because none of them is Lotte, all of them have tastebuds with which to savor the soup, and their palms joined in prayer are warm instead of cold, and in unison their six voices murmur the syllables to bless the food. Each and every second of that evening is an epiphany because no one's mother, rocking silently back and forth in the corner, reminds them that none of them is Lotte, but that on the contrary all of them are precisely who they are, utterly alive and vibrant, with their limbs attached to their bodies, their mouths full of teeth, their stomachs soothed by warmth and succulence.

Swan Lake has broken off in the middle of a phrase. Emil's breathing is rapid and even.

But why do we have so many enemies — what did we ever do to them — why do they keep flying over us, trying to burn us and kill us?

Saffie doesn't know to whom she can put these questions.

Clambering onto her mother's lap, she cuddles up against her — mountain mother, forest, ocean, sky mother, universe mother holding Saffie in her universe arms, the way she used to when she was little, why can't one stay little forever — "Is it true the men who want to kill us are the devil?" That's what the neighbor women say, they say the enemy is der Teufel, that he has fiery eyes and bullet-shaped teeth and that his hideous rumbling weapons were forged in the bowels of the earth — he comes from far away, his hatred of us is implacable and irrevocable, he wants to wipe us off the globe, annihilate our cities, our factories, fields, and railroads, he flies over us almost every night, sowing death and destruction, making our walls vibrate, our lamps and windows tremble and crack, the roar of his plane gets closer and closer, then moves away, then comes in close again: near — far — near — far —

Saffie strokes her sleeping child's cheek with her index finger. Even today she has trouble with distances. An object or a person standing several yards away from her can suddenly loom up huge and blurry, abnormally close, whereas a tree trunk directly in front of her will seem to recede and sharpen into focus at the same time, every etched detail of its bark attaining an unbearable clarity.

The children are awakened in the night by the siren's scream. They come creeping into their mother's room one by one, joining little Peter in her bed. One night, after the usual humming and whistling and pealing and crepitating, they hear — or rather they *receive,* less in their ears than in their very flesh — an explosion.

And, immediately afterward — silence.

They go back to sleep, tangled higgledy-piggledy in the big bed.

The mother gets up, puts on her bathrobe and slippers and cautiously steps outside to see what damage has been done. Other mothers are peering about. Who? Whose house this time? How many dead? Ah no. It's the devil's plane that's crashed — look — it's lying over there in the middle of a field, burning.

Saffie draws the sheer white curtains and leaves the room in which her son is sleeping. Pulls the door shut behind her.

Stands motionless in the hallway, arms at her sides.

The next morning she wakes up early — startled awake, perhaps, by the first cock's crow from the neighboring farm. Opening her eyes wide, she sees the other children deep in slumber all around her, and her mother stretched out in her bathrobe at the foot of the bed, sheltering the baby in the curve of her body, her cheek resting on a rough cushion. Leaning closer, Saffie sees that she's smiling in her sleep.

She is filled with an inexplicable sense of elation. Alone in the world! The only one up, with the sun shining out of doors and her heart beating in her chest! She extricates herself from the mass of tangled limbs, moving brothers' arms and sisters' legs with great care, it's like playing Pick-up Sticks — gently, gently! careful now! — the thing is to pick up this stick without making that one move — Lotte was good at Pick-up Sticks because she had long pointy fingernails, which gave her an advantage, maybe if God had let his nails grow long and pointy he would have been able to move the roofbeam when Lotte's house collapsed, but . . .

Saffie stands motionless in the hallway. Tomorrow. Raphael will be coming home tomorrow. Late morning, he said.

Snatching her dress from the back of the chair, Saffie slips on a pair of old sandals and finds herself outside. No one can see her. Never has she had the world to herself like this! She breaks into a run — for the pure pleasure of feeling her legs move, her heart beat, her body throb. She skips on one foot, then on the other, invents a game of hopscotch, runs backward, attempts a cartwheel, flubs it as usual and giggles at herself. . . . Freedom! Though she wouldn't know the word for it, that is the sublime sap flowing in her veins this morning.

All the houses are sound asleep, even the cows are still dozing in the fields, all facing in the same direction, if they fall ill now they have to die because her father is in Leverkusen, but before long he'll be coming home, before long the war will be over and life will go back to the way it was before. . . .

Ah — there's the wreck of the plane that crashed last night, a smoldering smoking mass of twisted metal — she runs past it, past the neighbor's farmhouse, and arrives at the barn just as the cock crows a second time.

Saffie is standing in the hallway, staring into the void, her arms crossed on her chest, both hands clutching her shoulders.

The barn door is opening. Slowly and creakily, the way doors open in dreams and in ghost stories. Frozen to the spot, Saffie stands there watching it. No one's pushing it, it's opening all by itself! Oh . . . yes, there is . . . not someone but something, a crawling red-black thing. . . . In a sudden gush of understanding, Saffie realizes — it's der Teufel, the devil, and at the same time der schwarzen Mann, the horrifying black man of the nursery rhyme who snatches little children from their beds at night and carries them off and murders them, *Wer hat Angst vorm schwarzen Mann?* Who's afraid of the big black man? He's dressed in the devil's khaki uniform but it's all filthy and torn and bloodstained, he's the one who tried to murder them in the middle of the night, his plane crashed and caught fire but he didn't burn, he can't die, all night long he's been lying here in the barn, waiting for her, knowing she'd come, and now he's inching toward her on his stomach, like a snake, his skin black all over, his red lips swollen, his red tongue lolling out, he's stretching out an arm toward her, his black eyes are bulging, staring at her, and now she can hear his voice as well, repeating the same alien word over and over, "Water!" he croaks. "Water! Water!" — the word of his black magic, the word for the death of her people — "Please, little girl! Please get me some water!" — panting, bleeding, sweating, stretching his arm out toward her — and Saffie, without a word, without a cry, without a thought — as cold and invisible as a thought — takes to her heels.

The news travels like lightning. Saffie, her mother, the neighbor women, the parish priest, the old men . . . all converge in front of the barn that sheltered the devil during the night. Armed with pitchforks and rifles, they surround him, vociferating and shaking their fists — but he just lies there in the entrance to the barn, his face in the mud, dressed in the burned and bloody remnants of his black devil's uniform.

Wer hat Angst vorm schwarzen Mann? He doesn't budge. He's not pretending. He'll never budge again.

That is the story her mother tells her later. But in her own memory-dream, or her own dream-memory, when Saffie runs home and tries to warn the others, her mouth forms the words — "Der Teufel! The devil! Over there! In the barn!" — but not a sound comes out. Her arms gesticulate wildly — "Over there! In the barn!" — but the others just look at her. "Poor thing," they say, frowning and shaking their heads. "Poor little thing . . ."

For the third night in a row, Saffie has had no sleep at all. When her husband's key turns in the lock, it's eight o'clock in the morning.

Yes, Raphael has decided to come home a little earlier than planned. He took the first flight out of Milan, burning with impatience to get back to his little family. Now, sticking his head through the doorway to the living room, he sees his wife huddled in one corner of the couch, her knees pressed together, staring at the radio, which is switched off.

"Saffie?" he says. "Is our Emil asleep? Is everything all right?"

She looks at him uncomprehendingly, in silence. Vaguely attempts to stand, then drops back onto the couch and sits there as if petrified.

"Tell me what you've been up to these past few days. . . . Was the weather nice? Did you get out a bit?"

Saffie's face and voice fill with confusion.

"Was the weather nice?" she stammers. "I don't know. . . . Maybe, yes. . . . How was it . . . where you were?"

"My love," says Raphael.

Kneeling next to her on the rug, he lays one cheek on her lap and encircles her body with both arms.

"I couldn't stop thinking about you two!" he says. "You can't imagine how much I missed you!"

"Me too," says Saffie after a pause.

"You look frozen. Would you like some tea? Let me make you a nice cup of tea. . . . Wait here, I'll be right back!"

Saffie waits.

Raphael returns with the tea, sets the tray on the coffee table in front of his wife, pours her out a cup, brushes her forehead with his lips.

"Thank you," she says — and adds, before tasting it, "It's delicious."

So nothing has changed, thinks Raphael. So she isn't getting any better. So motherhood isn't helping.

Disheartened, he goes and takes his bag of toiletries out of his suitcase, then locks himself in the bathroom for a shower and a shave. When he returns to the living room, he finds Saffie in the same position as before. Her tea, untouched, has gone cold.

Meanwhile, Emil has woken up. Judging from his plaintive cry, his diaper must be soaked.

. . . .

Every person's suffering is the most important, isn't it? Right at the moment, Emil's suffering is caused by a wet diaper, by uric acid eating into his crotch and buttocks. Don't make fun, now. You were in this predicament once yourself, and you may very well find yourself in it again some day.

VIII

Springtime settles in, other birds come to peck and twitter in the lovely courtyard of the Rue de Seine, the climbing ivy sprouts tender pale-green leaves.

The Milan concerts having gotten rave reviews, a prestigious concert hall in Paris calls Raphael Lepage's manager to say they'd be delighted if the great flutist could give a solo concert there in April.

Raphael's success in his professional life makes his private difficulties even harder to bear. In a burst of willfulness, he takes photos of his wife and son and sends a selection of them (including the only one in which Saffie is smiling) to his mother in Burgundy.

Things *must* work out, he tells himself. We must put an end to this dreadful paralysis. If we don't take action now, the situation can only get worse. There's absolutely no reason the three of us shouldn't be happy together. *Saffie, I beg of you — exist!* This is a marriage, it's for the rest of our lives, my son needs a real mother to talk to him, sing to him, teach him about the world. *Saffie, darling! Please come back to my bed!*

They haven't made love since the first weeks of her pregnancy. He doesn't rush things. He holds her in his arms at night and does his best to soothe her, reassure her, make her trust him. He speaks to her and touches her caressingly, and when he finally enters her, it's with such extreme gentleness that he's on the verge of tears. And Saffie . . . obeys him. No more, no less. Starts not-sleeping at his side again, instead of not-sleeping in the library. Keeps her nightgown on when they make love, so he won't see her stomach with its hideous toothy grin. Apart from that, she accepts him back into her body. Brings him to orgasm in the usual way, distractedly. Smiles at him and talks to him without being present behind her smile, her words.

Such is the (admittedly less than brilliant) situation in the Lepage household toward the middle of April 1958, the day of Raphael's first solo concert. The day everything is going to change.

At around ten in the morning, Raphael is practicing a piece he intends to play as an encore on his bass flute. This unexpected change of instrument is a gift he wants to bestow on the audience — abandoning the Louis Lot, the virtuosity and brilliance of tone with which he will have been dazzling them all evening, he'll play something grave and pensive on the Rudall-Carte . . . and after that they'll have no choice but to get up and file out of the concert hall in silence, to allow the sublime notes they've just heard to go on vibrating in their hearts and minds.

But in the middle of the piece he's working on, Raphael's bass flute produces a goose note.

"Damn!"

He breaks off, furious. He knows exactly what the problem is. The pad sticks when he takes his left index finger off the C key, so that the ensuing C-sharp only reiterates a wheezy, rasping C. This has been the Rudall-Carte's weak point ever since he bought it. It's a bit like an old lady whose left ankle sprains periodically — there's no way around it, you have to take it in to see a specialist.

Of course, he could abandon the idea of playing that particular encore on that particular instrument — the piece isn't even mentioned in the program — but he'd hate to do that. Once Raphael has formulated a wish, if only to himself, he can't bear to see it thwarted. Moreover, as we've just seen, he's in a particularly willful frame of mind these days.

Suddenly he has an idea — he can send Saffie to get his flute repaired. The instrument maker lives in the Marais, on the Rue du Roi de Sicile — not too far away. She can go there on foot, taking Emil with her in the baby carriage. It's a fine spring day, the walk will do her good. . . . Yes, Raphael definitely thinks this is an excellent idea.

Can never resist the pleasure of killing two birds with one stone.

Poor soul.

The baby carriage is parked next to the concierge's lodge on the ground floor. A huge, black, unliftable contraption. Saffie slips her silent living package into it. Hidden beneath the blankets at Emil's feet, the bass flute takes up more room than he does.

Pushing her baby carriage, the young woman moves off in the direction of the river. Never has she taken Emil farther than the Rue de Buci market and back. This is different — a real expedition. Raphael has drawn a map for her. You go down the Rue de Seine, walk under the entryway to the Académie and cross the Pont des Arts. The Pont des Arts is one of the most colorful and charming footbridges in Paris — it's full of blind accordionists and pipe organ players who perform with monkeys on their shoulders, and artists in smocks and berets who stand at their easels painting the Pont Neuf, the lush green triangular tip of the Ile de la Cité, or, in the distance, the twin towers of Notre Dame.

Saffie moves robotlike through the fragrant, heady air of the spring day. Locked in their respective silences, mother and son are equally impervious to the beauty that surrounds them. Here, looming up ahead of them, is the grandiose Louvre, and the refined if grimy Gothic facade of the Saint Germain d'Auxerrois Church — but Saffie doesn't so much as glance at them. She consults the map, which she's unfolded and laid out on Emil's coverlet in front of her. Turns right. Walks along the Seine — boats, barges, fishermen, loafers, lovers, other mothers pushing other baby carriages . . . All of it's invisible to her.

Emil is wide awake. His eyes are resting on his mother's face, but she doesn't notice. She's following the map.

She doesn't bat an eyelash as she approaches City Hall and a series of giant sand dunes come into view, with dozens of neighborhood kids careening down them, using them as slides. Nor is she impressed by City Hall itself, with its turrets, its statues, its fountains, its red-white-and-blue flags. She doesn't ask herself what historical characters and events might have given their names to the streets she walks down next — Pont Louis Philippe,

Vieille du Temple, Roi de Sicile — they're names, that's all. She checks them against the names on her map — yes, that's it — and turns accordingly — left, right.

Now, as she walks, the city grows gradually darker. Buildings black with soot, walled-up doors and windows, potbellied houses leaning on crutches. The streets are far narrower here than in the Odéon quarter, and far more crowded — barrows, carts and handcarts, trucks and wagons vie for space in the street. . . . The air vibrates with the screeching and squalling of children, the humming and hammering of machines, the monotonous calls of salesmen hawking their wares . . . the noise is invasive. To say nothing of the smells — sharp, pungent, acrid, exotic. . . . It would be natural for Saffie to feel disoriented — or, at the very least, curious. But no. She's doing her duty, following her husband's instructions, looking for the address, the right number in the Rue du Roi de Sicile, utterly oblivious to the throbbing teeming hectic atmosphere into which she's just plunged. There it is — far end of the courtyard — glass door with a printed sign in the window saying "Wind Instruments" — she knocks. Were she to glance left, she'd see that a whole wall of the place is made of glass, that this is a workshop, and that in the display window . . . However, as she has knocked, someone has come to open the door. Saffie enters, pushing the baby carriage clumsily in front of her.

Despite the wall of glass, it's darker in the workshop than outside, and at first all she can see are shadows. A tall shadow, skirting the baby carriage, goes to shut the door behind her.

Saffie-Duty is ready. She recites the speech she has prepared, pronouncing each word as clearly as possible.

"Good afternoon, Sir, I am the wife of Raphael Lepage, he apologizes to not come and see you himself, he prepares a concert for tonight and so this is an emergency, his bass . . . flute . . . his bass flute has a problem, he explains to you where it is, he wrote to you a letter about it, I have it here, in . . ."

Saffie stretches out a hand to rummage beneath Emil's blanket, but the stranger's voice stops her in midgesture.

"Ah! Ta-ta-ta-ta-ta-ta-ta-ta! Stop! *Not one movement!*"

She freezes. Not even surprised. It's always like this. You always have to expect the worst. Her arm drops back to her side and she closes her eyes. Gives up. Withdraws deep inside herself.

The man laughs. Not unkindly. With embarrassment, rather. He's disconcerted by the result his joke produced.

"Sorry," he says. "A silliness. A joke of silliness. It's because, you know, in Algeria, the mothers often carry bombs in the place of babies, under the shawls, in the food baskets . . . So it was just to laugh. I frighted you. Forgive me. Nice to meet you, Madame Lepage. Forgive me. I have met your husband once. A great musician. Please, show me the instrument. Sorry, yes? András," he adds, extending his right hand.

How can he make up for his blunder? The woman still refuses to smile; she hasn't said a word since he interrupted her spiel.

"Let's see, let's see," says András, bending over the baby carriage. Nimbly extracting the baby from under the covers, he cradles it in his arms and examines it attentively from head to foot.

"So. What's the problem with Raphael Lepage's instrument? Where is it broken?"

At this point, something incredible occurs: Saffie's cheeks turn flaming red. More incredibly still, she laughs. It's the first nonsarcastic laugh we have heard from her; she's been repressing it for so long that it sounds like a bark.

András raises his eyebrows, causing five deep furrows to appear on his forehead. Saffie herself is taken aback by the noise she's just produced. She takes a large gulp of air and shuts up.

"Hmmm . . . another silliness," mutters András, setting the baby back down in its carriage. "She is fine, that one. Very beautiful. Perfect shape, even if I can't hear the sound."

"It's a boy," Saffie says.

"Ah. Yes. And the other one . . ." says András, withdrawing the Rudall-Carte, setting it on his workbench and snapping the case open. ". . . It's a boy also?"

Again Saffie feels mad laughter rising in her throat — but manages to choke it back.

"Flute is feminine in French," she says, her voice even deeper than usual because she's fighting to control it.

"Oh, never mind. It's no use, I can never learn the genders. Why a flute should be like a woman and a table like a man, I can't understand."

"No, table is feminine, too," says Saffie — and chortles in spite of herself.

András reads Raphael's note.

"Yes, yes, yes, yes, yes," he says, scratching his head.

And looks at Saffie — really looks at her — for the first time. She lowers her gaze instantly, turning scarlet again.

"You're from what country?" she asks him, her eyes scanning the floor, taking in a thousand fascinating objects, dirty rags, cigarette butts, bottle caps, pieces of cork.

"*András* — what do you think?" says the man.

Already he's unscrewing the defective C key and prying out the pad. . . .

"I don't know."

"You don't know?"

"No," says Saffie, her heart thumping inexplicably.

"And Budapest, you know?" says András.

". . . Ungarn?" ventures Saffie, timidly, like a pupil being quizzed by her schoolmaster.

"Ah?"

This time András raises only one eyebrow, and keeps his gaze trained on the guilty key. Apart from the raised eyebrow, nothing in his demeanor betrays the churning of his heart. Though he's known the German language since childhood and mastered it to perfection, he has vowed that not a word of it will ever cross his lips again.

"You're also not French?" he asks. "You speak so well."

"No, not so well."

A pause. She doesn't want to say it. She says it. Softly.

"I'm German."

A pause. The pad András has pried from the key falls to the floor and stays there. András begins to whistle under his breath.

"Five minutes, it takes," he says at last. "Please have a sit, over there. . . ."

He nods vaguely in the direction of a stained, ripped and decrepit leather armchair, with springs and stuffing bursting out, on which a dusty pile of newspapers is presently enthroned.

"No," says Saffie. "I'm fine standing."

The silence between them returns, and grows so meaningful that the background noises become sharply audible by contrast. A radio is playing somewhere in the room — turning her head, Saffie sees it on a shelf in the corner. Likewise covered with dust. Emitting jazz and static. Saffie is having a hard time breathing. She's forgotten all about her son. She doesn't notice that Emil has fallen asleep, and that every time he exhales his upper lip trembles faintly. She's exploring her surroundings — her eyes dart this way and that, rejoicing in the disorder.

András's workshop is a wonderful mess. A proliferation of machines and tools and musical instruments, whole and in parts. In the window — a glittering jumble of flutes and saxophones, clarinets and oboes, trumpets and trombones. On the shelves, on the walls, on every available flat surface — little brushes and large balls, curving cylinders of gold, silver, and wood, flasks of oil, plastic boxes, labeled drawers containing springs and screws, keys and stops, bits of cork, felt pads. At one end of the room — a portable gas stove, a flame-blackened pot, a dirty dishtowel, a not very clean sink, a toothbrush glass, a teapot, packets of tea and sugar, a pot of jam, a dangling sausage, several jars of pickled cucumbers and red peppers. On the floor, on every table and chair, stacked every which way — newspapers, books, records, reams of sheet music. Finally, forming a wall at the opposite end of the room — a red woolen blanket suspended from the ceiling on nails . . .

Saffie's eyes roam around hungrily, stopping only when they reach the clock on the wall across from her — My God! *Six-thirty?!* The clock must have stopped. . . . No, the second hand is moving, Saffie can distinctly hear it ticking. Six-thirty! And Raphael was supposed to leave for his concert at six — it's just not possible! Fighting against her rising panic, refusing to accept that five hours can thus have dropped into the void, she consults her own wristwatch . . . and almost falls to the floor in relief.

It's only one-thirty. She has all — all — all the time in the world.

She directs her gaze, not toward the baby carriage in which her son is fast asleep, but toward the workbench where the Hungarian is seated, head down, whistling under his breath and fiddling with her husband's flute. There, her gaze comes to a halt.

Indeed, it could be any time at all.

The man is probably a few years older than Raphael. Unkempt reddish blond hair, already graying at the temples. Face lined with wrinkles. The rays of a half-sun appear at the corner of each eye when he smiles, lighting up his entire face. Woolen sweater with holes at the elbows, baggy canvas trousers, dark blue apron. Thick, oil-blackened, but graceful fingers, manipulating the gold-plated body of Raphael's bass flute.

Emil goes on breathing in and out, Charlie Parker goes on jiving in the static, the clock goes on ticking sarcastically, insisting on its ludicrous message, claiming it's now six-thirty-two — in the morning? in the evening? — warning them, in any event, to be careful — yes — time is passing, time is passing. . . .

Saffie is twenty-one years old and, in the past two minutes, she's undergone a total metamorphosis. She feels invested with a sacred power — the power to love this man and to make him love her. Standing there amid his marvelous mess, it's as if she'd passed not through his doorway but through his skin. Her thoughts are in a state of disorder, too. Her mouth has gone dry and desire is stiffening her limbs. Her green gaze is a powerful beam of light, scouring every square inch of the instrument maker's face and body. She says nothing. She stares at András — and, although it's a mystery, although no scientific theory has ever come up with a satisfactory explanation of the phenomenon, András, half turned away from her, head down, feels her staring at him.

Each and every one of his pores asks — *What? Really? Seriously?* And all of them answer in unison — *Yes.*

His fingers — his intelligent, thinking fingers, which understand musical instruments the way a gastroenterologist understands his patients' stomachs — his thick but quick, agile fingers . . . begin to slow down.

They slow down.

Saffie notices it. Her beam of green light grows still more powerful and intense. She's utterly concentrated in her gaze on this man with the blackened fingers, the baggy trousers, the graying temples. After a while, under the impact of her green gaze, András's fingers, hands, and arms stop moving entirely. He's petrified. Unlike Saffie, he hasn't forgotten about the child who is sleeping right next to them. He knows that if he looks up at the German woman before any more words are exchanged, he'll be lost. He casts about for something to say and can't come up with a single word, in any language.

He looks up.

Saffie's gaze is a ball of flame that blasts through his pupils and plunges to the depths of his stomach. He's on fire. He stares at her, this Madame Lepage of whom he knows nothing, not even her first name — and, staring at her, his eyes contain not the least trace of a question.

They stay this way. For so long that it would be impossible to feign innocence afterward, even if they wanted to. But they don't want to. They want only one thing — each other; to be united. Saffie is still standing; András gets to his feet and removes his apron. Crosses the narrow space that separates them and takes her hand — doesn't slip his hand into hers but rather *takes* Saffie's hand, from the outside, like an object. Draws her across the room with him, turns over the printed sign ("Back Soon," says a handwritten scrawl on the other side), and locks the door. (Oh that sound, Saffie! The sound of András's key turning in the lock! Did you ever hear more beautiful music in your life?) Leads her to the far end of the room. Floating at his side, Saffie radiates love like a nuclear aura, turning the air around her body blue.

Still holding firmly onto the German woman's hand, András pushes aside the red blanket.

.   .   .   .

This is where the instrument maker sleeps. His bed — a tangle of sheets and blankets on a ramshackle foldout couch — is welcoming in the half-light. Next to the bed — an old record player, a pack of filterless Gauloise cigarettes, an ashtray. On the back of one chair — two or three shirts. Hanging from a nail on the wall — a frayed gaberdine. On the shelves — more stacks of records and books, sheet music, newspapers. All this is his, all this belongs to him, to András. Beneath their feet — a rug of a type commonly found in North Africa, braided with the remnants of colored cloth.

They're standing face to face. András has finally let go of Saffie's hand. His left hand moves up to her neck. Between his thumb and curled-up fingers, still black from work, he unceremoniously pinches a thick piece of Saffie's neck flesh.

At this point, Saffie does something unexpected. She takes an initiative. Breaking away from the man's grip, she lays both her hands on his waist — a full, fleshy, carnal waist, much thicker than Raphael's — and starts moving downward. Her hands slide over the man's hips and thighs, she's kneeling in front of him and he's hard, still shut away inside his trousers, and she presses her face against him there, nose, cheek, eyelids, bone of eyebrow arch, pressing hard, then licking his trousers, prolonging the pressure of her tongue against the rough, dry material. . . . András, not closing his eyes, sets his two hands on the head of this perfect stranger, this foreign woman whose green eyes are now pressed tightly shut — and his touch sets off the first orgasm of Saffie's life, a violent wave that convulses her entire body, then flings it to the floor.

After a moment, András bends down to pick her up. Lays her on his unmade bed and sits down next to her, on the possibly Tunisian rug. He studies her angular features, still contracted from the intense pain of her pleasure. Then he gets up and moves off — goes back into the other world, the world beyond the blanket, where he turns off the radio. Returns — yes, András! András, returning! to her! — and bends down again, this time to put a record on the record player. (He purposely chooses something gay and frivolous — an Offenbach operetta.) Turning toward Saffie, he lights a Gauloise and powerfully exhales the first puff of smoke.

Saffie's eyes follow his every movement. Something in her gaze has changed. It looks more open than before, and more vulnerable. Stretching toward her the hand that's not holding the cigarette, András slowly but roughly runs the knuckle of his thumb under her chin.

"And she has another name," he says with a wide grin, "this German Madame Lepage?"

Again, Saffie laughs. A peal of free, spontaneous laughter. And replies, as her laugh comes to an end — or rather cries out, in a sort of savage joy, "*Saffie!*"

Startled awake by the sound of his mother's voice, Emil begins to wail.

The couple — oh yes, they're a couple already, and they'll remain a couple for a long time — get up and go back into the workshop together. Neither of them has removed a single piece of clothing.

"He's hungry?" asks András.

Saffie glances, not at her son, but at her watch. It's only two o'clock, and his last meal was at noon.

"No," she says. "It's too early."

She starts rocking the baby carriage to quiet him down — but the wailing only worsens.

"He has a character like his mother," says András. "I see it in his face. Amazing, really amazing. How old?"

Incredibly, Saffie hesitates.

Then says, "Two and a half months."

András has taken an old fob watch out of his pocket. Holding it a few inches above the child's face, he makes it swing back and forth like a pendulum. Emil's eyes instantly focus on the object, then start to follow it. His wails diminish in volume, grow fewer and farther between, finally cease.

"It's a boy," says András with a professorial air. "You know, if the watch goes in a line it's a boy. In a circle, a girl."

Saffie giggles.

"So you do have a watch for telling the time," she says.

"No," says András. "I only keep it in my pocket. I don't care what's the time. It's from my father."

". . . He's dead?"

András is still gently swinging the watch above Emil's face. There is a long silence.

"Yes," he says at last. "He's dead."

"And what . . . what did he do?"

"Same thing, wind instruments. But he was punctual."

"Ah!" says Saffie, laughing. And then, after a pause: "My father was a doctor for animals."

"Ah," says András.

His features relax imperceptibly. She used the past tense.

"*Ve-te-ri-narian*," adds Saffie, proud to remember a word Raphael taught her a few months ago.

Reassured by his mother's smell and by the sound of her voice, Emil heaves a sigh and goes back to sleep. The instrument maker leans toward Saffie across the baby carriage and brushes her dry lips with his.

"You will come?" he says.

He means *come again,* and Saffie has understood him.

"Yes," she says, her heart pounding like the bass drum at the end of *Don Giovanni.* "I will come."

Their eyes hold each other.

"The flute is okay," says András at last.

He tries it, his lips in contact now with the metallic mouthpiece, instead of Saffie's lips.

The C-sharp is perfectly distinct from the C.

"Your husband can play it tonight."

He snaps the case shut and slides it beneath the baby's blanket. Taps Emil's nose once, then Saffie's, with the tip of his index finger. Opens the door for them and accompanies them across the courtyard as far as the building's entrance. They exchange not another word, but András's eyes remain glued to the German woman, following the shape of her body as she moves away down the Rue du Roi de Sicile. She turns back to look at him just before she's engulfed by the crowd, and the pact between them is sealed. In cement.

Raphael's bass flute is repaired, and his marriage is in ruins.

IX

Meanwhile, the French army in Algeria has systematized torture as a means of interrogation, and capital punishment as a means of reprisal. Concretely, what this means is that innocent young French boys fresh out of secondary school are being taught to make young Arab bodies jerk spasmodically by attaching them to the electrodes of a magneto and throwing the switch; this treatment is flippantly referred to as "rock 'n' roll." They are also being taught to hold the alleged terrorists' heads under water for as long as possible without eliminating them as potential sources of information; this is known as "the breast stroke." And those draftees who find it difficult to demolish their fellow creatures in this manner — those who weep, protest or vomit — are mocked and humiliated, called chickens and cunts; they will be trained to bear it whether they like it or not.

Refusing to bow to these intimidation tactics, the FLN fighters pursue their campaign of surprise attacks, in the course of which their French enemies (and also their Algerian enemies, whether traitor harkis or rival MNA fighters) regularly find themselves relieved of their noses, heads, genitalia, or intestines. On May 13, 1958, deciding that the French government has been pussy-footing around long enough, overexcited generals foment a coup d'état in Algiers, paratroopers take over the radio station and the Government General building.

The situation is critical. Charles de Gaulle realizes this and decides to do something about it. After an eleven-year absence from power, he agrees to take France's destiny in hand once again.

Hortense Trala-Lepage also realizes it, reading the *Figaro* day after day, and begins to tremble for her precious vineyards overseas.

Virtually everyone realizes it — both in Algeria, where Muslim women tear off their veils, and in metropolitan France, where enormous crowds march down the streets chanting, "From Dunkerque to Tamanrasset — ONLY ONE FRANCE!"

Raphael, on the other hand, is removed from the crisis. He's traveling.

From now on, thanks to the remarkable reparation of his bass flute, and thanks to the resounding success of his solo performance in the prestigious concert hall, he'll be increasingly taken up by his career. He's now an absolute master of his instrument. All over the world, those who attend his concerts are mesmerized by the unique way in which he manages to combine passion and precision. Invitations come pouring in and he accepts them all, taking on concerts and workshops, tours and master classes that oblige him to leave Paris, often for faraway destinations, often for weeks at a time.

He takes on these engagements all the more readily as his wife is finally beginning to show some signs of contentment. Every time he returns to Paris, he notes that Saffie takes an obvious pleasure in going out for walks with the baby, that a blush of color has come into her cheeks and that a bit of flesh has fastened itself to her bones — and he rejoices. Thus, catastrophically serene in the knowledge that his wife and son are living together in a bubble of felicity, he continues climbing into taxis, trains, and airplanes that take him farther and farther away from the Rue de Seine.

Someone else notices Saffie's happiness and draws diametrically opposed conclusions from it — Mademoiselle Blanche.

The concierge is struck by a new buoyancy in the young woman's walk. She recognizes her step — a springy, irresponsible step, utterly unencumbered by the weight of reality. She herself used to walk this way — when, working as a secretary in a large company, she'd fallen head over heels in love, for the first and last time in her life, with a married colleague. Their story had ended badly — Mademoiselle Blanche had been naive enough to think the man could only make love to her because he'd lost all feeling for his wife. . . . Since he already had two sons, and since she wasn't yet aware of the havoc wreaked on her hormonal system by the acids of Saint Ouen, she'd dreamed of giving him a daughter. Then one day her lover had invited her to an office party to celebrate the birth of his daughter . . . and she'd almost died of shame and misery.

Yes, adultery can give you wings. As a general rule, the flight is brief and the fall brutal. And yet, watching the young woman move off toward the Seine with her baby carriage, Mademoiselle

Blanche's heart warms in spite of herself. It's not easy to advise caution to a person in the thrall of such blatant happiness.

All you can do is hope the damage will be limited.

András doesn't have a telephone. In the Marais quarter in the late 1950s, people who ask for a phone line are put on a two-year waiting list. But András isn't even on the list — he has no more use for telephones than he does for watches. This implies a certain passivity on his part — it's Saffie who will take the initiative for all of their meetings, without being able to give him advance warning.

On her second visit, she goes with the intention of taking her clothes off, and of having him take off his. Upon arriving at the glass door, however, she hears voices — and realizes, with a twinge of disappointment, that he's not alone.

He welcomes her naturally, helps her steer the baby carriage inside. Introduces her to his visitor, a tall, gangly black man —

"Saffie, Bill . . ."

"Hi, Saf!"

Involuntarily, imperceptibly, Saffie recoils. Not since the devil in the barn has she found herself less than ten paces away from a black person. When he holds out his hand, she sees the other hand stretched out toward her and the word "Water!" flashes through her mind — it's been years since she learned the word's meaning, but its aura of menace has never disappeared — *Wer hat Angst vorm schwarzen Mann?*

Getting hold of herself, she raises her own hand and watches as the black man grasps and shakes it.

"Have a seat!" adds András — and, turning his back on Saffie to make her feel perfectly at home, he picks up the thread of his conversation with Bill, in English.

So it's as simple as that. In spite of the baby carriage and in spite of the baby, she has the right to be merely "Saffie" when she comes here. Her life in Germany no longer exists; nor does her life on the Left Bank — she can say, do, be anything she wants. She is free! Seeing a newspaper lying on the floor, she picks it up, settles into the misshapen armchair and pretends to read. Almost ten minutes go by before she notices that the newspaper is printed in Hungarian. She smiles at herself. The two men are standing next to the workbench and chatting calmly. As far as she can tell, the instrument maker's English is even less fluent than his French. They light cigarettes, leave them lying in ashtrays, try out half a dozen saxophone mouthpieces one after the other. Emil wakes up and Saffie changes his diaper, then goes back to the armchair and waits, without impatience. Simply, with happiness. At last the American gives himself a shake, gets to his feet, picks up his instrument and ambles over to the door, followed by the Hungarian.

"So long, Saf," he says. And, giving András a light, friendly punch on the arm, "See you around, man."

András closes the door behind him. Turns the sign over in the window. Turns the key in the lock.

"This man is a genius of tenor sax," he says. "You come with me one day, to hear him?"

"Yes," Saffie replies, her voice low, cracked, almost broken with desire. "I'll come where you want, András."

"You say it well, my name."

(The Hungarian "András" is a harsh, powerful name, with the accent on the first syllable, the r rolled on the palate rather than in the throat, the s pronounced sh. . . . Our "Andrew" is quite insipid by contrast.)

Hand in hand, mouth on mouth, they go behind the red blanket.

He has removed all her clothes, as she had hoped he would. He has removed all his clothes, as she had hoped he would. He has lain down next to her on the bed, his member stiff and swollen, to contemplate the whiteness of her body. He has slowly run his fingers along the nasty sneer left by the scalpel, then traced the perpendicular stitches one by one. It's as if he himself had just engraved the length of barbed wire on the skin of her stomach.

"From the baby?" he asks.

Saffie nods. And murmurs, "I can't have any more."

The two half-suns burst into being at the corners of András's eyes. "Ah . . . ," he says. "That's one problem less!"

Bending over her, he catches one of her nipples between his lips, teases it with his tongue and begins to suck on it powerfully. And Saffie feels something she's never felt before — it's as if a second bloodstream were coursing through her veins, as if she were twice as much alive — because, from the depths of her body, this man has drawn a few drops of mother's milk, the milk the pediatric nurses had peremptorily told her she'd never have. Tasting the sweet lukewarm liquid on his tongue, András has swallowed it. He has drunk from both her breasts — and now, as they stare into each other's eyes, their bodies unite.

In the midst of their loving, Emil begins to cry. He isn't wailing the way he did last time, he's truly crying. At the age of three months, his eyes secrete real tears. One wracking sob leads to another, and before long his face is crimson and congested. At the far end of the room, beyond the blanket, his naked mother is swooning beneath the instrument maker's rough hands, his massive body, the slow repetitive thrusts of his sex. She rears up, her entire body arching then dissolving. She, too, is weeping. She climbs on top of her lover, her face bathed in tears and sweat. Droplets of salt water fall from her forehead onto his face and she licks them off. András speaks into her ear — brief, rough words in Hungarian which she doesn't understand but which transport her. The child shrieks with impotent rage.

At last, the man who will not impregnate her, the man who will spill his seed on infertile ground, the man whom she loves and will love forever, the man whose weight and strength inside of her, on top of her, make her almost delirious, founders on her shore with a great cry, then another. Saffie has long ceased to count the breakers submerging her.

He gets up first. Yes. It's András who goes to pick up the baby, half-strangled by its sobbing, and returns to lay it between them in the bed. Recognizing his mother's smell, Emil turns to her and calms down at once.

"Look how he loves his mother," says András.

Saffie lays a hand on the infant's head. Her palm fits itself to the delicate curve of its cranium. She slides her fingers through its soft black curls, so much like Raphael's. András's words have sent a strange thrill rippling through her stomach.

"You're so handsome," she says to András in a murmur.

"No," says András. "You. You are handsome."

.   .   .   .

April drifts into May. Saffie is floating on a cloud of love, and her son is reaping the benefits. When she handles his body to dress him, bathe him, and feed him, her gestures are more caring and attentive than before. The tiny boy begins to trust her.

Raphael, when he happens to be in Paris, delights in watching them.

Nothing has changed in their intimacy — Saffie is as passive as ever in her husband's arms — but, Raphael tells himself, there's no point in focusing on the negative. Our marriage is no worse than many others. Martin and Michelle, for instance, are constantly bickering about money. . . . Whereas — look at my wife and son — they're positively basking in joy!

And indeed, Saffie is happy. She has gone to the *Bon Marché* department store and purchased window boxes and parti-colored geraniums for their living room windows. Now, with Emil propped up on velvet cushions on the rug next to her, she's standing bare-armed at the window, gently tearing away dead leaves. She feels the delicate spring wind on her forehead, smells the fragrance of flowers she herself planted. She's fully conscious of every moment — aware of the white arc of her arms in the air, the sensation of her fingers palpating the leaves. . . . This *is* happiness, isn't it? I, in any case, know no better definition of it. Her head is no longer the dark closet we sojourned in a while ago, teeming with terrors from the past — it has become a place in which it's possible to live. Saffie has finally learned to embrace the present, because every second of the present brings her closer to her next encounter with András. And although she still has bouts of insomnia, there are also nights when she sleeps in unprecedented peace.

Waking up on the morning of May 29, the day de Gaulle will officially be offered the job of heading the French government, Saffie is again surprised to find that the light switches aren't working. Another power strike! There's no way she can light the gas flame to sterilize Emil's baby bottles. Well, too bad . . . at the age of four months, her son will just have to swallow a bit of cold milk!

She feels lighthearted and gay, because Raphael is in England — and tomorrow, Sunday, she plans to take Emil over to see András.

"Right, my little one? Right, baby Emil? We'll go visit András tomorrow, won't we?"

András has a surprise waiting for them — a canvas bag he's made himself, with a complex system of straps so that Saffie can carry the child on her stomach.

"But . . . why?"

"Because! Today we make a trip!"

And he points to the far corner of the courtyard, where a tandem bicycle is leaning against a wall next to the communal toilets. A genuine antique, all iron and black leather. A miracle.

"I found it last week, in the eleventh arrondissement. In a . . . a shop of old junk."

"András!"

He climbs onto the front seat of the bicycle, Saffie settles in behind him with the baby . . . and they set off. Utterly content to be pressed up against his mother's body and rocked by the bicycle's rhythmic roll, Emil falls asleep almost at once.

"Where are we going?"

"The flea market!"

András loves to wander through the open-air stalls of Clignancourt — he often comes across bits of machinery that can be adapted to the needs of his profession. Today, however, the expedition is cut short. Only halfway to the Porte de Clignancourt, on the Boulevard Barbès, their path is blocked by a group of military police. The entire area is cordoned off; the streets are empty and deserted, the air leaden.

András stands there, balancing the bicycle and studying the scene, his brow distorted by a deep frown. Saffie sees his jawbones working and realizes he's grinding his teeth.

"Why? . . ."

She can't even finish her question. Just the sight of men in uniform turns her to stone.

"What, why?" snaps András. "It's Algeria. You don't read in the papers?"

Saffie remains silent.

"You don't know?" András insists. "*There's a war, Saffie.*"

"No . . ."

The word escapes from her lips before she has time to think. There's a war: *No.*

"Saffie. You live in a country at war. France spends a hundred billion francs each year to fight Algeria. *You even know where it is? Algeria?*" says András, almost shouting now.

Emil starts in his sleep and clings to his mother more tightly. Blanching, Saffie puts her arms around him and lowers her eyes.

"The war is over," she says in a nearly inaudible voice.

"No! The war is not over!" cries András. "From '40 to '44 France lets Germany fuck her in the ass and she's ashamed, so in '46 she starts a war in Indochina. In '54 she loses this one too, the Viets fuck her in the ass and she is ashamed, so three months later she starts a war in Algeria. You don't know?"

Saffie keeps her head down, rocks her son, says nothing.

The silence between them grows painful. Finally András shakes his head abruptly and lights a Gauloise. Turns the tandem around. Heaves a sigh filled with rage and smoke, and starts pedaling back toward the Marais.

Their first outing — a failure.

They won't go riding on the tandem again for the rest of the summer. Frenchmen and Algerians are found with their throats slit, their arms and legs chopped off, their rib cages crushed, their genitalia in their mouths. Bombs explode in various parts of the capital. Police stations burn.

Furious at seeing her gracious being thus abused, Paris deploys the full panoply of her armed forces to protect herself. Algerians (and those who are so unlucky as to resemble them) are subjected to identity checks at every step. They're plagued, pestered, harassed, arrested on the slightest pretext, beaten, insulted, whipped, stripped, taken in, rounded up, sequestered by the hundreds in the Japy Gymnasium or the former Beaujon Hospital — just to make sure that they feel at home in this country, since after all — if only they'd acknowledge it — it's theirs.

Raphael, who is about to leave for a tour in Latin America, cautions his wife not to venture too far from home. Since every traffic intersection in the city center is now bristling with armed soldiers, Saffie is hardly tempted to disobey. From June to September, she takes Emil to the Marais workshop only twice, and then, briefly. The rest of the time, she dreams. Daydreams. Talks to András in her mind. Asks him questions and laughs out loud at his answers. Stands naked in front of the mirror in the afternoon heat, gazing through lowered lashes at the reflection of her body, caressing herself and imagining that her hands are those of András. Looks after her baby, her flowers, her housework.

Toward the middle of August, Emil learns to sit up all by himself. Saffie claps her hands, congratulates him with a kiss, proudly announces the news to Raphael over the telephone.

So you see, Saffie has reentered the realm of the living. She no longer treats her baby like a package. For the time being, at least, she has joined the ranks of fussing, cooing parents. Just like them, she follows her offspring's foreseeable progress in a state of ecstasy — noting, for instance, that Emil is able to roll onto his back from his stomach and vice versa — or to lift his heavy head and follow her with his eyes.

She has become a virtually normal mother.

On the other hand, Emil's serious stare and the rarity of his smiles remain abnormal. It's as if he were obsessed with something he should not, at his age, have to understand.

X

Summer turns to fall. Realizing that the recent wave of violence in metropolitan France is doing considerable harm to their image, the FLN and the MNA decide to calm things down a bit. The military presence in the streets of Paris grows more discreet, and by mid-September Saffie decides she can allow herself the luxury of an entire afternoon in the Marais.

Upon reaching the Rue du Roi de Sicile, however, even she who never notices anything is forced to notice something. Hundreds of people are buzzing and eddying around her disturbingly; the crowd is so thick she has a hard time ploughing through it with Emil's baby carriage. Floating above the pavement are millions of white feathers. Running down the gutters — rivulets of blood. Vibrating in the air, absurd and frightening — a chaotic chorus of squawks. . . . Saffie feels the icy hand of fear clutch at her guts. Tense and sweating, she shoves the baby carriage forward roughly, drawing angry insults from women clad in black. By the time she reaches the instrument maker's courtyard, she's on the verge of hysteria.

Fortunately, András is there alone. He takes her in his arms and studies her face — what's wrong?

"What's going on, outside?" she asks, her voice almost a squeal.

"Oh!" says András, relieved. "It's nothing. A holiday!"

"I thought I'd never . . . I . . . with the carriage . . . It was horrible. What holiday? Why are they killing chickens on the sidewalk?"

"Yom Kippur. The Day of Pardon."

"I don't know it. A French holiday?"

Stunned, András stares at her.

"Saffie," he says, after a long silence. "You don't know?"

She shakes her head. No, she doesn't know.

András's features harden. He seizes her arm and drags her back outside, leaving Emil alone in the workshop. Strides down the street with her, so fast she can hardly keep up — she trips and slips in the filth; before long her shoes are smeared and filthy with chicken feathers, chicken entrails, chicken blood. He drags her down the whole length of the Rue des Ecouffes, where the turmoil is more appalling still — pungent odors, raucous cries, abrupt laughter, opaque epithets — it's a nightmare, she's in pain, the viselike grip of András's hand is hurting her, she longs to stop up her eyes, her ears, her nostrils, why is her lover putting her through this torture?

They arrive at the Rue des Rosiers.

There, releasing her arm at last, András hisses at her vehemently, "*Look, Saffie! . . . Look! . . . Saffie, look!*"

Says no more. Stands there and waits.

Reluctantly, hesitantly, the young woman makes an effort to decipher the reality laid out in front of her eyes. The blue, red, and green storefronts of the Rue des Rosiers. Weird calligraphy, candelabras, stars, printed signs covered with thorny symbols . . . and, yes, young boys wearing embroidered skullcaps . . . women in wigs . . . older men with dangling sidecurls . . . beards, caftans, broad-brimmed hats . . .

She feels ill. Can neither speak nor breathe. Doesn't dare to so much as look at András. Feels the ground giving way beneath her feet.

András puts an arm around her shoulders and they start moving again, far more slowly than before. Finish their walk around the block. Return to the Rue du Roi de Sicile by way of the Rue du Ferdinand Duval, formerly the Rue des Juifs.

It's over. András has pulled the glass door shut behind them. Emil is awake, but not crying.

"They're . . ."

Saffie has never pronounced the word in French before. She has heard it, though. She heard it countless times on the lips of Monsieur Ferrat or rather Julien, in the summer of '52, in the course of his merciless lessons in love and history. Now she pronounces it.

" . . . Jews?"

András makes no answer. He has relaxed considerably. Whistling under his breath, he goes over to the kitchen corner and puts on a pot of water for tea. The absurd clock ticks and tocks. Saffie, feeling feebler by the second, drops into a chair and waits for the room to stop spinning around her. When she's able to speak again, her voice is no more than a whisper.

"But you . . . you . . . you're Jewish, too?"

András snorts with laughter. He turns to her, laughing, all his features creased into a smile that's half affectionate and half sarcastic. Seeing Saffie blush in confusion, he stops laughing and clears his throat.

"Nowadays, Saffie," he says solemnly, "when Germans ask Jews are they Jewish, the Jews want first to know why the Germans ask the question."

Silence. Then —

"Saffie . . ."

More silence.

"You're Jewish? *You?*" she repeats, in a somewhat more assured tone of voice.

He watches her study his face, then blush at being caught studying his face, then study it again, as the face of the man she loves.

"You . . . you're *Jewish?*" she says for the third time. "And . . . you love *me?*"

András nods. Just once.

"I didn't hide something," he says.

Saffie smiles, gradually overcome by a weird euphoria. When she speaks again, her voice has recovered its depth and throatiness.

"No," she says. "I didn't hide something either. . . . I didn't tell you I was a virgin."

"Because I could see right away."

"See what?"

"That you're a virgin."

They move toward each other. Embrace. Kiss with a fresh ferocity. Go behind the red blanket together on shaky legs, forgetting all about the water that's simmering on the flame. When they come back into the workshop, the water has evaporated and the pot has begun to burn.

"And you didn't see anything . . . Saffie, you disappoint me. You're not observing. You don't look around you in the street, you don't read the papers, okay, it's not good but I can accept. But *this!*" (Feigning indignation, he slaps a hand to his crotch.) "It's not the same! *My* prick, my beautiful prick who loves you so much — you could think it was a goy prick! No, that makes me mad. . . . What can I do to punish you? I don't know what you deserve, to be so . . . so not observing."

"It's because I don't look at it with my eyes," says Saffie, coming over to where András is seated and gently squeezing the soft bundle of flesh in one hand. . . . "I look at it with everything, everything but my eyes. So forgive me. On my knees I beg you."

She kneels down next to his chair and kisses his feet.

"Forgive me. . . . It's the Day of Pardon, no?"

András's laugh cracks like a whip.

"You . . . do you believe in God?" asks Saffie a while later, cradling Emil in the crook of her left arm and spooning mashed bananas into his mouth.

"No," says András. "No, nobody in my family. For a long time. We never went to synagogue. God doesn't exist and we, we're his . . . how do you say? His favorite people. An old joke. Very old."

As the autumn weeks slide by, the lovers carefully exchange bits and pieces of their past. Only bits and pieces. Watching their words. Treading with extreme caution on the mined fields of their memories. Each of them dreading the moment when the other might utter a sentence that would be fatal to their love.

Saffie learns that András arrived in Paris only two years ago. There had been a revolution in Hungary in the fall of '56 — the people wanted a less rigid system of government, independent from Moscow. The uprising had lasted a mere twelve days — and was crushed by the arrival of Soviet tanks.

"My mother said go, go far away, today the border is open and maybe tomorrow closed, so go! Go to France!"

"But not her?"

"No. She prefers to stay in the house with her memories, not put a big pack on her back and go running in forests and jumping on trains and hiding."

He'd escaped from Hungary with his best friend Joseph — but the latter, dazzled by Vienna's flashy shop windows, had decided that Austria was fine with him and refused to go any farther. András, unable to bear the sound of the German language, had pushed on as far as France, taking with him nothing but his old gaberdine and a backpack crammed with the tools of his profession. The weeks of fear and hunger and cold, the diarrhea, the ice-crusted fields, the waiting, the endless black nights, the inhospitable Alps, the dozens of encounters with policemen, border authorities and innkeepers, the phony papers, the phony smiles, the perpetual lack of truth and trust . . . Appalled, he realizes that all this can now be summed up in just three words, the names of three countries —

"Austria, Switzerland, France. My mother has a cousin in Besançon, she gave me some money to start."

"But why did she want you to leave?" asks Saffie.

"Because, in Hungary, it easily can start all over like before, for the Jews. It's a very super ultra Catholic country. . . . You're a Catholic?"

"No," says Saffie. "Yes," says Saffie. "Before. Now I don't know. Nothing, I think."

András learns that one night, to take Saffie's mind off the noise of strafe bombing, her mother had described to her in lavish detail how she would be dressed on the day of her First Communion.

White satin gown, white taffeta veil, a crown of white flowers in her hair . . .

But it had never happened.

"She's still alive?"

"No. And your mother?"

"Yes . . . in Budapest."

   .   .   .   .   .   .

The next time:

"Why Paris?" asks Saffie.

"Oh, Paris . . . It was my mother's dream. The City of Light in the country of Enlightenment. . . . Ha! Paris is dark and dreary. Also filthy. No?"

"Yes. Disgusting."

They laugh.

"And you?" asks András. "Why Paris?"

"My professor when I was in high school, in Tegel. He said France is the country of freedom."

"Ha!"

   .   .   .   .   .   .

The time after that:

"And your father," murmurs Saffie, "he died. . . ."

"Yes. With my uncle."

". . . The Germans?"

For a fraction of a second, András hesitates. Should he tell her? His four grandparents, yes. Thirteen of their children and grandchildren, yes. The Nazis took a while to get around to Hungary but once they got there they did the job with their usual Gründlichkeit: starting in May of 1944, all the Jews in the provinces, whether Hungarian-born or refugees from Eastern

Europe, had been sealed away in ghettos, and during the summer (with Paris already liberated!), all four hundred thousand of them had been sent to slaughter. Plus a hundred thousand gypsies. Eichmann had emptied the country out . . . but was brought up short upon reaching Budapest in the month of August, the Red Army having just crossed the border. Late that fall, a homegrown Hungarian fascist party known as the Arrow Cross seized power, and from then on it was a free-for-all. Absolute terror. The end of the line for the two hundred thousand Jews still lying low in the capital's ghetto.

Why should I tell her? thinks András. After all, I could just as well invent a different life story for myself. A story in which Saffie's people wouldn't have gassed mine. A story in which I would have had no uncles and aunts and grandmothers and grandfathers to begin with, each with their specific shape of nose, curve of neck, color of eyes, crinkles of laughter, bullets in brain, face crushed by boots . . . A story in which I wouldn't even have been born in Hungary, and my name wouldn't be András. . . . Why should I tell her the true story instead of the made-up one? Just because it happens to be true? How does this truth concern her? Must she really be forced to learn it? *Which* truths are we required to pay attention to, and which can we ignore? Am I allowed not to give a shit about what happened this very morning, but on the other side of Earth — or on this very spot, but in the year 1000? Has Saffie ever even heard the *word* Hiroshima? *What*, says András to himself, still in the same fraction of a second, *are we allowed not give a shit about?*

"No," he answers in a slow, bitter voice. "My father isn't killed by the Germans. I'm not angry against the Germans. I'm angry against everybody."

Thus, he tells her only a part of the story — the part about the two brothers, his father and uncle, arrested one day in late December when they'd ventured outside the ghetto to scavenge for food. As deportation was no longer possible, the city being completely surrounded by the Soviet army, the Arrow Cross had come up with their own method of exterminating Jews. They tied them together by the wrists, two by two, then led them to the edge of the Danube; and there — a bullet a pair. No wasted ammunition. The dead body dragged the living one into the water.

András has never known which of the two, his father or his uncle, received the bullet.

"What about you?" asks Saffie, after a long silence. "What happened to you and your mother?"

András and his mother owe their lives to a communist concierge, who concealed them behind a coalpile in the cellar of an Aryan house — certified Aryan, guaranteed Aryan, bearing the official Aryan plaque — while the city of Budapest was decimated by the collision of the two monsters, the Wehrmacht and the Red Army. . . .

"Like Berlin between the Americans and the Russians," says Saffie.

András says nothing.

"How old were you?" Saffie goes on.

"Seventeen."

"So . . . only thirty now?"

"Thirty, yes."

"I thought older. At least thirty-five."

"Yes, I know."

Another day:

"And you . . . your father, he died how?"

"His brain, an attack. . . . Three years ago."

"You were sad?"

"I don't know. . . ."

András asks no further questions about Saffie's father.

"And your mother . . . she died how?"

Long silence. Nearly a month will elapse before Saffie answers.

They live at a remove from the world, and this enhances their perception of the world. Gradually, from one week to the next, the scales begin to fall from Saffie's eyes.

"Look, Emil!"

Emil can now sit up straight in his baby carriage. At age ten and a half months, in a mad attempt to catch a pigeon in the Place des Vosges, he takes his first steps. Saffie and András applaud wildly. Passersby take them for a normal couple, out for a walk with their son. But they're abnormal — abnormally free and happy. With amused detachment, they watch the poor French people go rushing across the park with their heads down, not even taking the time to admire the superb russet monochromes of the autumn leaves.

There's no hurry. They're immersed together in their own time. András has no fixed schedule — he can work at night if necessary, and sleep during the day. The minute Saffie crosses the Pont des Arts, she ceases to be Madame Lepage, the famous flutist's wife (a role she has learned to play convincingly when she accompanies Raphael to dinners or gala concerts) — and surrenders herself utterly to the universe of her love.

They go for walks in the streets of Paris, often and at length. Even when it rains, they walk and talk, sit down on park benches, muse in silence, then get up and walk again. They have a preference for the north and east of the city — the Faubourg Saint Antoine, the Père Lachaise cemetery, Belleville. . . . Instinctively, they avoid the streets around the Saint Lazare train station and the whole Left Bank, which they associate with Raphael. When weather permits, they climb on the tandem bicycle and ride out to the Buttes Chaumont Park, with Emil snuggled in his canvas bag between Saffie's breasts. Sometimes, using public transport, they venture far beyond the city limits — into a weird landscape of high-rise apartment buildings and vacant lots, rutted roads and endless skies. They stand there doing nothing, staring at the passing trains, the poignant thrust of factory chimneys, the low thick swirls of smoke.

But most often they simply walk together, pushing the baby carriage. Their love makes every paving stone in the city gleam, puts every object in its place, confers a glaze of perfection on every facet of reality, even the peeling walls and insalubrious courtyards of the Marais.

One day in November, they're sitting on a tombstone in the Père Lachaise cemetery gazing down at the Menilmontant rooftops, their slate tiles glimmering gently through the fog, and she tells him. About her mother.

It only takes a few words. It's possible to pronounce them, if someone's there to hear them. András is there.

Saffie saw the whole thing. She was in the kitchen with her mother, who was doing the ironing. Not an electric iron — the old-fashioned kind you had to keep heating up on the coal stove. Saffie was folding the clothes as her mother finished pressing them — her younger brothers' and sisters' little shirts and dresses. She was the eldest daughter. She had an older brother, but he wasn't there at the time.

"He was where?"

"I don't know exactly. He was eleven, three years older than me."

"Hitlerjugend?" asks András in a neutral tone of voice, his eyes fixed unswervingly on the glimmering rooftops of Menilmontant.

"Yes," says Saffie. "Yes, of course. When you turned ten you had to join, you had no choice. So he wasn't at home and I was the oldest, at eight. And then the Russians come. My mother and I hear their boots on the front door. My mother sets the iron on the stove. She rushes to see where the little ones are, to find a place to hide them. I don't know . . . where. . . . The Russians, there are four of them, they have rifles, all of them are shouting at once, I don't understand what they're saying. They grab my mother and throw her down on the kitchen floor, right in front of me. They take the hot iron from the stove and press it . . . here, on her chest. There are two of them on top of her. She doesn't scream. She is . . . you know, holding her teeth together tightly, so the little ones won't hear. . . ."

Saffie rises, goes over to the baby carriage to make sure Emil is asleep, and returns to sit next to András on the gravestone. Her eyes are dry.

"They? . . ." asks András.

"Yes."

"You, too?"

"Yes."

"And then, after . . . they kill her?"

"No. No. She kills herself. Six months later. In November, just like now. Because everyone can see she will have a baby, and my father . . . he came home only in September."

Propping his elbows on both knees, András leans forward and covers his face with his hands.

"She kills herself?"

"Yes. After the Russians, she's not the same. She's like . . . like a woman in stone. She never sings anymore, she hardly speaks, and at night we can hear her crying. . . . It's Peter who finds her.

He's about Emil's age now, a little older. He goes into the kitchen, you know, like this, crawling on his hands and knees, and he finds her. . . . He thinks she wants to play. He tries to stand up, to catch her feet in the air. . . ."

Several long gray minutes go by, in silence. Saffie realizes she's still breathing, still drawing the damp misty air of Paris into her lungs.

"Many people," she goes on at last, in a low voice. "Not only my mother. In our neighborhood . . . at least five or six that I know. They turn on the gas, or they hang themselves, or they take poison. . . . And then, the woman next door comes to look after us. Frau Silber, the mother of my friend Lotte who died. Her husband . . . he died too, on the Eastern Front. But . . . I don't know . . . my mother must have told her about the Russians. . . . She . . . Frau Silber . . . she's very hard on me. She whips me with her belt . . . on my back, on my face . . . I think she's afraid because . . . because of what happened, so . . . she's afraid I'm bad. . . . She keeps me away me from the other children, especially my sisters. . . ."

"And now?" asks András. "Where are they now, your sisters?"

"I don't know. It's over. I don't know."

Again she takes a deep breath, inhaling the cool and humid Paris air. She is here.

"And you?" she asks. "Brothers and sisters?"

"No," says András. "The only child."

"Your mother must be sad?"

"Yes. I think so."

Later, in the fine warmth of the workshop, Saffie bends over the baby carriage to change Emil's diaper. Standing next to her, András watches as she wipes the baby's buttocks, then blows on his stomach to make him laugh. As he studies the child's tiny genital organs, his face slowly hardens and his eyes take on a faraway look. Sensing the change in him, Saffie looks up.

"My mother," says András, "when I left, she told me . . . if I had a son, not to . . . you know . . . to cut him . . . there."

"She said that? Why?"

"So . . . if one day it all starts over again. So they can't know he's a Jew. You know, they say — it's better a Jew with no beard than a beard with no Jew."

Saffie laughs, deeply moved. Lowers her eyes. Kisses her son on the midriff again. And murmurs to him, "You hear that, Emil? You hear what your father said? We're going to leave you *just the way you are!* All right?"

And she lays a teasing finger on his foreskin.

Christmas is drawing near.

On December 21, Charles de Gaulle is elected president by a landslide: sixty thousand of the eighty thousand presidential electors (universal suffrage is still a thing of the future) vote for the man who has promised to restore order in Algeria.

Raphael purchases a Christmas tree — as he'd said he would, during Saffie's pregnancy the year before — and then, ransacking every closet in the house, he digs out all the baubles, garlands, and figurines left over from his childhood.

His mother still refuses to meet the intruder. (She has framed the photos of her grandson, tossed the ones of her daughter-in-law into the fireplace.) It's a pity, thinks Raphael — in fact it's a tragedy — but if that's the way she wants it . . . The Lepages of the Rue de Seine are now a family in their own right; they'll celebrate Christmas together.

Saffie buys the ingredients for pastry and spends two long afternoons in a floury apron, making Lebkuchen and Stollen the way her mother used to do, decorating them with icing sugar, slivered almonds, and candied fruit. Then, borrowing an *Elle* recipe from Mademoiselle Blanche, she bravely embarks on a turkey flambé with Cointreau.

The evening is a success. Sweet, submissive and wifely, Saffie has no trouble keeping up her end of the conversation, commenting on the gossip from the music world that Raphael shares with her and laughing at all his jokes. Emil, enthroned in his brand new high chair, is silent and uncannily still throughout the meal, as if hypnotized by the candles.

On Christmas afternoon, marveling at the changes wrought in his wife over the past year, Raphael goes off to join his orchestra for a concert at the Champs Elysées Theater. And Saffie goes off to join her lover.

.   .   .   .   .   .

András has fashioned a mobile for Emil out of spare flute and saxophone parts. He's suspended it from the ceiling, directly over the spot near the stove where Saffie parks the baby carriage. By pulling on a string, Emil can jerk into motion the brilliant metal keys and rods. Wriggling and gurgling joyfully, he pulls the string over and over again — gold, silver, rhythm, tinkle, glint.

They're on the couch — the old foldout couch whose springs creak and whine with their every movement. Saffie is stretched out full-length, her head on András's lap, and they're listening to a 45-record someone has just given them — Schubert jazzified by the flutist Hubert Laws.

Saffie closes her eyes and András traces her profile with the tip of his index finger. Beginning at her hairline, he moves slowly down across her forehead and between her eyebrows, following the narrow ridge of her nose and sliding into the delicate groove between the base of her nose and her upper lip.

"This," he says, "is where the angel puts a finger on the baby's lips, just before it's born — *Sshh!* says the angel — and the baby forgets everything. All it learned before, up in paradise — forgotten. So it can come into the world innocent. . . ."

Languorously, Saffie opens her eyes to check the mark of the angel on her lover's face — but her gaze is instantly drawn upward to his eyes, to the dancing of their blue light as he studies her.

"Without the angel," András goes on, laughing, "*who* wants to get born? Who could agree to come into all this shit? Ha?! Nobody! A lucky thing there's the angel!"

"And when do people stop being innocent?" Saffie asks dreamily, her lips barely moving beneath András's finger. "What about you? Are you innocent?"

András doesn't answer. His finger resumes its downward path, lingering for a moment in the little hollow between Saffie's lower lip and chin, then following the curve of her chin and the fine straight line beneath it, pressing against the top of her neck and the slight bulge of her Adam's apple, and diving at last, in slow motion, into the intimate sensuous grotto between her collarbones.

"You know," he says — Laws has stopped playing, but the record continues to spin around and around, the needle scratching its empty grooves — "the first time I saw you . . . I know something about you. . . ."

"Ah? You knew who I was?"

"No, no . . . Not that. . . . But I see you and I think — ah. Here's a woman, I tell myself, who . . . who never knows nostalgia."

"Nostalgia?"

"You know . . . when you're here and not here. You get up at night, you go drink some wine in your kitchen at Paris, and suddenly you remember another night, before, when you were in your country. I don't know, a piece of music, or . . . somebody's hand on your hair — or a tree, maybe, your favorite tree. . . . All that is far away, in another life, and you're here, standing in your kitchen in Paris. You open the window — and there's the sky of Paris, the smell of Paris — but you, you're in the other night, the other place, and . . . but . . . your life . . . You don't understand."

Frowning, Saffie stares at him and shakes her head.

"You see?" says András. "I was right."

XI

In every tale of passion there comes a turning point. It can happen sooner or later but as a rule it happens fairly soon. The vast majority of couples miss the curve and go careening off the road, flip over and crash into a wall, their wheels spinning madly in the air.

The reason for this is simple. Contrary to what you'd believed during the first hours, the first days, at most the first months of the enchantment, the person you love hasn't radically transformed you. When you miss the turn, the wall you run into is the wall of your Self. Yes, there it is again — every bit as nasty, as petty and as mediocre as it was before. You haven't been magically healed. Your wounds are still raw. Your nightmares begin again. And you're filled with rage at the other person — because as it turns out, you *haven't* undergone a metamorphosis, love *hasn't* solved all life's problems, and you're *not* floating ecstatically heavenward — but rather, as usual, pulling your own weight down here on Earth.

The turning point between Saffie and András is marked by no incident in particular. It's a gradual rather than a sudden thing. But in the winter of '58–'59, their old demons begin to stir like bears in springtime and go bumbling about in the dark caves of their souls.

Ah. So the dragon hasn't been vanquished by the pure, shining blade of the other person's love. The monster's still alive. . . .

This morning, a morning in January, the weather prevents them from going out for a walk. Blustery gusts of rain and wind.

Emil is standing on a chair next to the wall of glass. With an absorption that is almost disquieting in so small a person, he's studying the patterns made by the raindrops as they run down the windowpanes. Part of the roof is made of glass as well, and he stares up at it, listening to the dense irregular beat of the rain, trying to understand how something so dramatic can be taking place so close to him without doing him any harm.

The radio is playing *"Qué sera, sera"* by Doris Day, still on the hit parade more than two years after its release. András is whistling along with the song as he gently takes an oboe to pieces. And Saffie, curled up in the ancient leather armchair (which she recently patched up with shiny black adhesive tape), is drinking tea and watching him work. András's hands have their own thought processes — they pick up the right tool, turn, twist, tap, grease, run carefully over the instrument's shining skin in search of a dent.

She doesn't understand.

This, perhaps, is the first hint of the turning point in their love — that morning, Saffie can't understand the calm patience with which András goes about picking up screws and pins and springs, mixing lac, cutting disks out of woolen fabric — his least gesture utterly attentive and precise — how can you —

Yes. Once again, in Saffie's head — unfinished sentences.

Hands have to be dirtied so that immaterial music can go wafting through the air, but how can you —

András adjusts the pad, fits it flush into the key, taps and presses it, picks up his tool again — oh such meticulousness, such loving accuracy — so that music — so that a sound — so that a note, someday, will be able to undulate for a moment in the air — such extravagant care, such fervent attention to detail, the all-but-invisible detail that will enable the note, someday, in the air —

"Whatever will be will be," wails Doris Day — and András, totally absorbed in his work, hums along with her — *"The future's not ours to see, Qué sera, sera, What will be will be."*

The following day, a day of First Communion, the village square gets hit. The little bodies are hastily carried off, their white dresses drenched in blood. All that remains is an empty space strewn with rubble and broken glass. Pulverized, the little church. Eviscerated, the school that Saffie and her brothers and sisters used to attend. In flames, the missals and the pews, the books and the blackboards. Twisted and melted, the organ pipes — and yet, thinks Saffie, someone had cared about the organ too, just as András cares about the oboe — someone had studied organ-building and paid fanatical attention to pipes and keyboards, stops and pedals — so that music — so that music — so that the notes of music in the air . . . why? . . . oh András, *how can you?* How can you bend over a musical instrument and calmly go on humming and tapping?

"When I was just a little girl, I asked my mother, what lies ahead?"

Gust blast burst blast gust, the organ pipes twisted and melted, the careful stores of wood and hay consumed in cracking stinking minutes — flames are still licking at the shacks and sheds — the blue sky is choked with gray and the only air left to breathe is ash.

Trees are suddenly, ludicrously visible from living rooms — you glance up — no ceiling — trees.

Saffie runs across the rubble-strewn village square, crunching broken glass beneath her feet — soon other children will come to join her and they'll go hunting for shrapnel together — and tomorrow, if enough water has collected in the bomb craters, they'll be able to catch tadpoles.

You shouldn't care about things so passionately, András, you shouldn't get attached, it's dangerous to take things so seriously, to want things so badly, András, András. . . . Saffie is adrift in a chasm of memory — and when Emil, dizzy from looking up at the rain on the glass roof, loses his balance and tumbles off his chair, she responds to his screams in slow motion, like a sleepwalker. It's András who leaps to his feet — gets there first — picks the child up and sits with him in his new rocking chair, crooning to him softly, *"I asked my sweetheart, Will there be rainbows. . . ."*

Saffie gives herself a shake and goes to join them. Bends over her son, but says nothing.

"Why don't you sing?" András asks her a moment later, when Emil has stopped crying.

Saffie blushes, as if he'd accused her of a crime — and as if, moreover, she was guilty.

"P . . . pardon?"

"Why don't you sing?"

He isn't even looking at her. He's rubbing the bump on the little boy's curly head where it hit the edge of a shelf.

"I . . . I . . . don't know the words," stammers Saffie.

"No, I mean . . . anything! You can sing to Emil."

"But . . ."

Again, Saffie feels she's under attack and needs to defend herself.

"But he's a French child!" she says, grasping at the first argument that comes to mind. "You see? And I don't know the words to French songs."

András knits his brow and says nothing. He continues rocking Emil and humming along with Doris Day until the song comes to an end.

Then he says, gently, "You're crazy! You can sing what you want! You're his *mother*, Saffie! He *loves* you! You have the right to sing to him in German."

"No!" says Saffie, more upset by the minute. "I sing badly, I don't know how."

András jumps to his feet.

"You're crazy!" he says again, this time not as gently. "A baby doesn't care about that. It's his mother's voice, that's all. It's *your* voice, Saffie, so for him it's beautiful."

Not in years — not since her failure at the Düsseldorf Welcome Hostesses School — has Saffie felt such paralyzing tension. She looks at her watch.

"I have to go," she says. "Come on, Emil! I put on your coat, we're leaving. . . . Say bye-bye to András."

András makes no attempt to restrain them. Doesn't accompany them to the porte cochère. Lets them go, and resumes whistling "*Qué sera, sera*" — whereas, on the radio, it's already time for the news broadcast.

．　　．　　．　　．　　．　　．

There they are.

At the turning point.

．　　．　　．　　．　　．

Raphael happens to be home that evening, and while Saffie is giving Emil his bath he bursts into the bathroom with his camera.

"Such a beautiful scene, Saffie!" he says, bombarding them with flashes. "I wish it could last forever! I wish Emil could always be a baby, and you could always give him his evening bath. I don't even know *why* it's so beautiful — it's like an image of paradise lost. You know what Freud says? There's no human feeling as pure and unambivalent as that of a mother for her male offspring."

Raphael recalls his father quoting this one day to his mother, to tease her about her immoderate love for her son.

"Unam . . . bivalent?" repeats Saffie tentatively. She's never heard the word before.

"That must be why every museum in Europe has at least a dozen paintings called *Madonna and Child*. I'd never given it any thought, but it's obvious — every man finds it easy to identify with the Baby Jesus, and every woman with the Virgin Mary!"

"Yes," says Saffie, absently.

Just then, leaning forward in the bathtub, Emil grabs a lock of Saffie's hair and says clearly, "Ma-ma."

"You see?" cries Raphael. "What did I tell you? You got it, son! *Ma-ma*. First try, right on the nose! *Ma-ma!*"

"Ma-ma," repeats Emil gravely, gazing into his mother's jade-green eyes and gently tugging at her lock of hair.

Saffie stares at him, transfixed. Then, crossing her arms on the edge of the bathtub, she lowers her head and begins to sob in silence. Emil slaps the surface of the water with the flat of his hand, splashing both of them and repeating excitedly, "Ma-ma! Ma-ma!"

Raphael is speechless. He'd worried about never having seen Saffie cry — and now, as if a giant thundercloud had burst inside her soul, tears are gushing from her eyes in torrents. For a moment, remembering the dismal, depressing months of her pregnancy, he winces with fear. Will she plunge again? Dear God, please, not that. . . . But maybe . . .

"Tears of happiness?" he murmurs.

She nods, sobbing harder still.

Overcome with emotion, Raphael helps her to her feet and puts his arms around her, crushing her to him.

"You're soaked from head to foot, my darling!" he says tenderly. "Between your tears and the bathwater. . . ."

Two days later, the rain has stopped falling and the city is in the grip of a harsh, metallic cold. Saffie returns to visit András — not out of desire this time, not even out of love — but out of necessity.

"Can we go for a walk? I have to talk to you."

András grabs his coat (the same thick warm gray gaberdine he was wearing on the night he fled Hungary) and they set out.

Rue Malher. Rue des Francs Bourgeois. The entire length of the Rue de Turenne. Rue Béranger. The Passage Vendôme, leading to the Place de la République. They buy a bag of roasted chestnuts at the foot of the statue, then take the Rue du Faubourg du Temple as far as the Canal Saint Martin. Sit down on a bench at the water's edge and eat the burning hot chestnuts. Toss the husks to the ducks, who don't so much as deign to look at them.

Emil is sitting up in his baby carriage, alert and wide awake, muffled against the cold. His dark little eyes shine out from amid the pastel hues of his woolen scarves and blankets.

Saffie senses the time has come. She can now tell András what she so desperately needs to tell him.

Oddly enough, she begins with the stuffed poodle.

"I only have one paw left," she says. "It was a present from my father. When I was a little girl, very little. Two or three."

Vati — a young man with laughing green eyes bending over to kiss his tiny daughter, all the while hiding something behind his back — and she, skipping and leaping around him, wild with impatience because she'd begged him to buy her a poodle that morning when he went into town — but the package was always in front when she was behind him and behind him when she was in front — "Give it to me! Give it to me!" she squeals, louder and louder because he's deaf in one ear, the left one, at mealtimes she always makes sure she talks into the right one, but now they are whirling so fast she can't be sure which ear her words are going into — "Gimme!" — Can't he *hear* me? — You never know when Vati can hear you and when he can't, Saffie's face is red and her body hot from running, she's about to explode with impatience — "*Gimme!*" — "Ah, ah, ah! What do you say?" "Please!" "Please, my handsome Daddy." "Please, my handsome Daddy!" "Please, my nice, handsome, smart Daddy." "Please, my nice, handsome, smart Daddy!" — at last, at last, he allows her to wrench the present from his hand and tear off the wrapping paper with her frenzied fingers — "Oh!"

The disappointment is overwhelming. It isn't a real poodle, only a toy. She should have known, but at age two she hadn't known, that people don't wrap real dogs up in wrapping paper. . . . She stares up at her father, her eyes filled with reproach. "But it's *better* than a real one!" he insists. "It can't get sick!"

"And you see," she says now to András, "I forgive him. I'm so proud of him. . . . He knows how to cure all kinds of animals. . . . The neighbors bring to our house their dogs and cats, their canaries . . . and they go away happy! Except if the animal is very old or very sick, and then they ask Vati to give it a shot. And even then they're happy, because Vati is so calm doing it, he tells them their pet didn't suffer. . . . So they thank him, they pay him, and they take the animal home and bury it."

A long pause.

András says nothing, nothing, nothing.

Barges go floating slowly down the canal, their chimneys occasionally grazing the upside-down Vs of the pedestrian bridges. Emil is captivated by the sight. "Oh!" he exclaims softly to himself, over and over again.

Just then, who should go walking down the far side of the canal but Michelle — the woman whose home Saffie stayed in at the beginning of her pregnancy. She's just come out of Saint Louis Hospital, where the doctors have informed her that her youngest child (a boy, not the little girl whose bed Saffie slept in) has kidney failure. Wholly absorbed by her anxiety, Michelle is walking with her eyes on the ground — and, as Saffie is staring into the swirling gray mists of her past, the two women don't see each other. This sort of thing happens all the time. We love telling each other about miraculous encounters, extravagant coincidences — "Small world, isn't it?" we exclaim, every time it happens — but in fact life contains a far greater number of missed meetings, near encounters, not-quite-coincidences.

"And then," pursues Saffie, "after the war . . . how can I explain to you . . . You must know, because of Budapest, but . . . you can't know."

Another lengthy silence, and finally she resumes, in a low voice. "We drink fear. We eat death. We breathe . . . how do you say . . . Blei, lead. Everything is so heavy! So heavy! The silence chokes us. No one is talking in the house. Mutti is dead. The children are hungry. Everyone is hungry. We live in the basement of our own house, and upstairs there are the French. How can we understand this? Little children can't understand. Why do we live in the basement of our own house? Why is there water up to our ankles? Why do we have no food, no medicine, no clothing, nothing? Why did Mutti have to go away? And the GIs in the street, they make fun of Vati, they push him off the sidewalk and spit at him with their chewing gum. . . . No one talks. Frau Silber talks only to give orders, or to pray. Everything is so tense, it's . . . schrecklich, horrible. . . . Can you understand, András?"

András has pulled Saffie's hand into the pocket of his gaberdine to warm it up. He strokes it with his left thumb, not answering.

"And then . . . and then, since no one has enough to eat, people can't feed their pets anymore, and they start bringing them over to our house. To my father . . . They stand in a line at the door, dozens of people, all carrying their pets to be killed, in a cage, in a basket, in their arms — and the poor animals aren't even *sick*! They're just hungry, like we are! I'm nine years old, and I see everybody crying, holding their dog, their cat, their hamster. . . . And now, they don't want to take them home afterward. There's too much death already. So Vati has to bury them. Every evening, he goes out in the backyard, he makes holes in the lawn with his shovel, then he puts the animals in and covers them. He says nothing. He never talks about it. Never. I think he's very, very tired. . . . But I . . . I can't just . . ."

Saffie represses a tremor. Takes firm control of her voice to keep it from sliding upward to the high notes of hysteria.

"I *can't* just leave them there! So, later in the evening . . . I sing to the animals my father buried. . . . Once . . . in August, the sun was going down . . . there was a big black dog, my father gave him a shot of cyanure . . . and he went mad, he was running around everywhere in the backyard, with . . . you know . . . bubbles here, at the mouth. . . . At last he fell down to the ground, he was panting. . . ."

Again Saffie has to stop to get hold of herself.

"And so, to help him die, I sang to him — a lullaby my mother used to sing when there was an air raid. . . . Listen . . ."

She sings softly, but her voice wavers in spite of herself, her eyes fill with tears and overflow, she brushes the tears away with an impatient hand and goes on singing. He must understand, András — he *must*, or they'll miss the turn —

"*Guten Abend, Gute Nacht, Mit Rosen bedacht, Mit Nelken besteckt, husch, unter die Deck. Morgen früh, wenn Gott will, wirst du wieder geweckt. . . .*"

Nauseous, she breaks off.

"Do you understand, András?"

Oh, he understands. He understands only too well. Brahms's Lullaby embodies everything he abhors about the German soul — its piousness, its sentimentality, its submissiveness. Yet he remains silent. Neither nods nor shakes his head. Has stopped stroking the German woman's hand with his thumb.

"It means . . ." She hesitates, preparing her translation. "Good evening . . . good night . . . covered with roses and . . . I don't know, some other flower.... Get in ... under the covers.... Tomorrow morning ..." — she's weeping again — "if God wants, you'll wake up again. It's *horrible,* you understand? Because flowers grow in the garden, so when you sing that to a child, it means she's going to die.... Every night when I went to bed, it was like getting into my grave — and in my dreams, the flowers on my bedcover got all mixed together and started to rot...."

Saffie presses her face to the sleeve of András's gaberdine — but withdraws it at once, for she hasn't finished yet.

"Sometimes, András ... the animals weren't buried well.... You know, my father was so tired, he didn't make the holes deep enough.... Then the earth moved, and they came back to the surface. I could see their paws sticking out.... When I went out in the backyard, it was ... like walking on a carpet of corpses."

At this point her stomach heaves, putting an end to her story.

On the nape of András's neck, on his back, his arms, his chest, all over his body, his hair is standing on end. Not out of sympathy. Out of revulsion. For Saffie's words have revived in his mind the image of other hastily buried bodies — not of domestic animals, but of Jews. As he's a voracious reader, as he can't help devouring everything he comes across, he's read this, too — the description of precisely the same scene, penned by the great Soviet writer Vassilii Grossman. Immediately after the war, Grossman had written about the fate of the Jews in the Ukraine, in his native town of Berdičev. Five mass graves filled with corpses — women and men, children and old people, every Jew in the village, hundreds and hundreds of corpses, including that of his own mother ... five enormous ditches. And then, the same words — the earth moving, the corpses swelling and starting to bleed, building up pressure, finally splitting open the earth's surface.... The soil of Berdičev was too clayey to absorb all the liquid, so the Jews' blood came seeping out of the graves and before long everyone was splashing about in puddles of blood; the Germans had to order the local peasants to add another layer of earth to the graves, then another, then yet another, because the earth kept heaving up and cracking open, releasing fresh streams of blood. . . .

Without their noticing, the icy humidity has filtered through their clothes. Saffie and András are chilled to the bone. Frozen — by the cold, and by the images that have sprung up to haunt their brains. They've ceased speaking. They no longer know that they're sitting side by side on a bench near the Canal Saint Martin, in the city of Paris, on a January day in 1959. Right now — drowning in the blood of their respective memories, drained of all hope and desire, engulfed by the immutable loneliness of suffering — they've virtually lost each other.

Fortunately, Emil is there.

He's having a bowel movement — his whole face reddened and distorted by the effort. Tears glitter in his eyes.

"Oh-oh!" says András, getting to his feet. "You choose a good time, my boy. So far from home, and you let go like that? Oh, we're in deep shit now, your mama and me!"

They walk swiftly back to the workshop, not talking but close, their inside hands joined and their free hands pushing the baby carriage.

XII

Visitors flock to the instrument maker's workshop for warmth in the winter — warmth from the coal stove if there happens to be coal on hand, and more dependably, warmth from the music and conversation. All sorts of individuals drop in to spend an hour or two drinking tea or mulled wine, trying out various instruments and chatting together in a weird assortment of languages — jazzmen from the United States, Yiddish violinists from Goldenberg's delicatessen (Saffie is amazed at how much their language resembles German), prostitutes and transvestites from the brothel down the street at n° 34 (run by a policeman's wife in flagrant defiance of the 1946 no-tolerance law), recent refugees from Central Europe . . . to say nothing of Madame Blumenthal, an obese little widow with a heart condition who lives on the top floor and stops off at András's every day at noon, her daily food purchases divided into two string bags, to gather strength for the dreaded climb upstairs. . . . Everyone, it seems, knows the way to the wind instruments workshop.

Saffie feels at home in the polyglot ferment on the Rue du Roi de Sicile. Speaking little but listening attentively, she serves tea to everyone and washes the glasses in the tiny sink afterward, proud to be perceived as the hostess of the place.

As for Emil — pampered, coddled, and caressed by dozens of foreign hands and voices — he soon comes to be known from one end to the other of the street as the Prince de Sicile. The minute his baby carriage lumbers into view, friends and acquaintances of András's crowd around it, bending over to inquire as to His Majesty's health. The child's first efforts at speech are a hilarious mixture of idioms. Fortunately, Raphael has no ear for foreign languages, and interprets Emil's bizarre exclamations — "Oy weh! Salud! Hey, man!" as the continuation of his baby babble.

These past few weeks, Emil has begun calling András Apu, which means Papa in Hungarian. And Raphael is Papa.

In other words, even as he learns how to talk, he's being taught how to lie.

Only twice in the course of that winter do András's visitors cause Saffie displeasure. No, three times — but the third time is so serious that the word displeasure is an understatement. The third time comes close to destroying their love.

One Wednesday morning in February, András goes out at ten o'clock to buy sugar for their tea, leaving Saffie and Emil alone in the workshop. Suddenly the door bangs open and in lurches a wild-eyed, hiccuping tramp, dressed in rags, reeking of wine, his twisted blackened toes visible through the holes in his shoes. Horrified, Saffie leaps to pick up Emil and press him to her body, staring at the man, unable to articulate a single word. The tramp, apparently as disconcerted by the young woman's presence as she by his, glances around the workshop uncertainly. "Where's M'sieur André?" he mutters, blinking his red eyes. "Ain't home, M'sieur André?"

Just then they hear András whistling in the courtyard. Saffie prepares a string of sentences in her mind to take the edge off the shock — I'm sorry, he came in without knocking, please don't be angry, he didn't threaten us or anything — but to her surprise, András doesn't bat an eyelash upon seeing the man.

"How's it going, Pierrot?" he asks, scarcely even looking at him.

More surprisingly still, he walks over to a bookshelf, slips his hand behind some books, withdraws a small leather purse and hands it to the tramp.

"There. . . . See you tonight! Have a good day!"

"Th-thank you, M'sieur André," stammers the man. And, bowing and scraping grotesquely, he backs off toward the door. "M-my humble respects, Madame!"

András shuts the door behind him.

"A friend," he explains simply. "He sleeps in the food market — the one at Enfants-Rouges, you know it? No? Rue Charlot? A big market with a roof on top, so at night the bums go up there to talk, and then they sleep all together between the boxes, to keep warm. But there are . . . you know, pickpockets. So when Pierrot has some money, he asks I keep it for him at night — because with the wine, he sleeps too well. He frighted you? Oh!"

Laughing, he puts his strong arms around mother and child, still clinging together.

"You're frighted, my love!"

"Apu," says Emil, twisting round to climb onto András's neck.

The second time, it's a woman.

Saffie sees her the minute she pushes open the workshop door — a blond curvaceous woman of about András's age, sitting where Saffie usually sits, in the wrecked armchair, the armchair she herself recently repaired — yes, the intruder's fleshy thighs are crossed over the black adhesive tape with which Saffie's own fingers patched up the torn leather — and András, seated at his workbench, is bent over a trombone.

Saffie is brought up short. It's as if she has stumbled into a movie theater playing the film of her life, with a different actress in her own role. A film in a foreign language with no subtitles — yes, András and the buxom blond are chatting together in Hungarian — and they still haven't turned to look at her. András isn't quite the same person when he speaks his own language, Saffie has noticed this before — he talks louder and faster than usual — right now his words are making the other woman laugh so hard that her breasts jiggle. . . .

Shock. The blood drains from our heroine's face. She's destroyed, a nonentity — just like the first time we saw her, standing motionless in front of Raphael Lepage's door.

"Hey! My Saffie! Come!"

András has seen her at last. He gets to his feet.

"Come! This is Anna!"

Saffie moves toward them like an automaton. Stick legs, stick arms, the jerky motions of a robot programmed to shake hands with human beings.

"Enchantée," says the Hungarian woman, with a heavy accent. "Enchantée" is probably one of the only words she knows in French.

Saffie can't. Can't. Simply cannot remain in the same room with this mature, intimidating woman, András's friend and compatriot, closeted with him in the unspeakable intimacy of the mother tongue. . . . His wife, perhaps? My God . . .

"I . . . I was just . . . passing by. I'm sorry!" she stammers, looking at her watch. "I'm late. I must go now. Thank you!" she concludes idiotically. "Good-bye!"

And she rushes off, struggling to maneuver the baby carriage through the doorway despite the fact that Emil, having struggled to his feet, is stretching out his arms to András — "Apu! Apuka!" The other woman, Anna, bursts out laughing and shrieks something in Hungarian — but Saffie doesn't understand her, she understands nothing, she wants only to be out of here, away from here, at once. . . .

András catches up with her in the courtyard. Takes her firmly by the shoulders and turns her around. Shakes her, as if she were a little girl.

"You're silly, my love. You know? You're silly."

The German woman's body is passive and lifeless — András has never felt it like this before — it's the body she usually reserves for Raphael.

"Anna is the wife of my best friend at Budapest," he tells her. "She's in Paris for three days with a little orchestra. She wants to give me the news from everybody. Stay! Don't be silly! Don't leave!"

"Is she Jewish?" asks Saffie in a low voice, her lips pressed together, every organ in her body convulsed with jealousy.

András flinches as if she'd slapped him.

"Yes she's Jewish. Of course she's Jewish. All my friends they're Jewish, at home. So what? You . . ."

"She looked at me," says Saffie, interrupting him, "with — with contempt. As if I was . . . nothing! A German Laus!"

Saffie doesn't know the word for lice in French. Neither does András, but he knows it in German, and it's a word he loathes.

"You imagine . . ." he says, slowly detaching his hands from Saffie's shoulders. He stands there with his arms at his sides, staring at her, shaking his head. "You imagine things. But don't stay, if you want. Don't stay."

She whirls around and stalks off, stiff as a poker, as Emil cries inconsolably in his carriage.

The third incident, the one that's all but fatal to their love, occurs a month or two later. They've seen each other on several occasions in the interval, and had time to patch up, smooth over, iron out their misunderstandings.

That day, Saffie and Emil get to the workshop later than usual. Raphael has just left for Geneva, after having spent more than a week in bed with the flu. Saffie nursed him like a good little wife — the way her mother used to nurse her when she was small — with hot, honey-sweetened lemonade, strained vegetable soup, melted lard-and-cinnamon poultices. She took his temperature morning and night, picked up his dirty tissues, changed his sheets. Smiling calmly, she reassured him over and over again, "Of course you'll be well in time for your concert Monday night — I promise you!"

When Saffie behaves in this manner, she's not being hypocritical. She doesn't need to force herself to be kind to Raphael. Think of all she owes him! Everything. It's certainly not András who could have given her a French name, and French nationality. . . . The idea of going to live with her lover in the Marais has never so much as crossed her mind. Even when her husband is away for long stretches of time, she wouldn't dream of spending the night at András's — he doesn't have a separate room for Emil; he doesn't even have a bathroom. He performs his weekly ablutions at the public baths on the Rue de Sévigné and does his washing once a month on the Rue des Rosiers, plunging his bundle of dirty clothes into the enormous bubbling vats of the wash house. He makes a meager income, eats scanty and irregular meals, owns neither an oven nor a fridge. Saffie isn't torn by inner conflicts. She likes her life the way it is — divided in two. The Right Bank, and the Left. The Hungarian and the Frenchman. Passion and comfort.

This is why, as she cared for her sick husband with quasi-maternal solicitude, she felt no impatience.

And this is why, the minute Raphael has gotten into a taxi headed for Orly Airport, his body stuffed with medicine and his soul soothed by a thousand whispered compliments, she finds it perfectly natural to turn to Emil and say, "Shall we go see Apuka?" — and they set out.

.   .   .   .   .   .

Mademoiselle Blanche watches them as they move off down the Rue de Seine. Ah yes, she says to herself, Madame Lepage still has those wings on her feet. Adulteries do last, sometimes — for years — even a lifetime. (Still, the boy is getting a bit big to be mixed up in all that. The concierge would be curious to know how he feels about it, what he does with himself when his mother is with the other man. But it's impossible to get the child alone — Madame Lepage never lets him out of her sight.)

.   .   .   .   .   .

The April sun is already setting, it's past seven o'clock and dusk is beginning to claim the city when Saffie and Emil finally reach the Rue du Roi de Sicile. Oddly, whereas the lights are on in the workshop and voices can be heard from inside, the glass door is locked. Well, that's no problem — Saffie has the key! She slips it into the lock, trembling with joy at the idea of seeing András again — and then, yes, she does see him — sitting at the kitchen table with his back to her, across from a man she doesn't know, a swarthy-skinned young man with black hair and a black mustache, eyes of fire . . .

Upon hearing her enter, both men jump to their feet, their faces contorted with rage — yes, András's too, contorted with rage. . . .

"What are you doing here?"

"What am I . . . I . . . what do you mean?"

Saffie plummets into silence. It's a bad dream — or else a bad awakening from the best of dreams. . . .

András seizes her by the elbow. Pushes her out into the courtyard. Shuts the door behind them. Doesn't so much as nod in response to Emil's elated cries of "Apu! Apu!"

"I'm sorry, Saffie," he says, and his voice is low but firm. "Today you can't stay."

"What is it? András, what's happening? Who is this man? I won't leave unless you . . ."

"Tomorrow, I tell you. You come back tomorrow and I explain. Now go. Please, Saffie."

Without waiting for her answer, he goes back into the workshop and shuts the door in her face.

Saffie goes all the way back to the Rue de Seine, not knowing whether she's walking, flying or swimming.

And, for the next few days, she sulks. But it's not easy to sulk when the other person doesn't have a telephone. Saffie's silences are many and varied; they can mean all sorts of things. How can she be sure András will interpret this particular silence as a reproach? He has no way of getting in touch with her. Doesn't even know exactly where she lives. Has never wanted to become acquainted with the details of her other life — the bourgeois life she leads with her husband the flutist.

But this same husband is scheduled to return on Sunday. And Saffie can't bear the thought of welcoming him if she hasn't first cleared up the situation with András. Thus, on Friday, she returns to the Marais.

.   .   .   .

András is alone. But not a bit more forthcoming on the subject of his visitor with the mustache.

"Who was it?"

"Who was who?"

"Stop it . . . you promised to tell me."

"Emil, look what I make you. . . ."

It's a flute — a nubbly green-and-orange gourd squash from the preceding autumn; András has dried it and drilled careful holes in it; now he breathes into it — three airy notes — and holds it out to the child. . . .

"*András!*"

"Saffie, you have your life, yes?"

"It's not the same thing!"

"Okay, it's not the same thing. You and me it's not the same thing, okay."

"But I don't hide things from you. . . . András, tell me! . . . Is it Algeria? *Is that it?*"

And, little by little, imploring, ardent, loving — oh yes, for Saffie is quite capable of resorting to feminine wiles when she wants to get her way — she succeeds in extracting information from him. Learns, indeed, rather more than she would have wished.

Learns that the man she loves believes in communism, just like the Russians who devastated her young body in 1945.

"I thought you were *against* the Russians! That's why you left Hungary!"

"Against the Russians invading my country. But Saffie, *all* Jews are Marxist, you don't know that? All except the hasidim.

And almost all Marxists are Jews, starting with Marx. Look — the best bolsheviks, Trotsky, Zinoviev, Kamenev, Grossman — of course! Because communism is the only one who says, Jewish or not Jewish, religion is a pile of shit, a commerce of lies, it belongs in the past, from now on everyone will be intelligent!"

The man's name is Rachid. András knows relatively little about him. Just that he's a leader of the FLN's French Federation, a fund-raiser, aged twenty-five. That he dreams of being able to study medicine and become a surgeon. That he's the eldest son of a large family, but that two of his brothers have already been killed, back in his home province of Constantine. That his mother worships him. That his father was shot to death in the Sétif massacres of 1945. (Saffie has never heard of this event — she was doing something else on May 8, 1945, when forty thousand Algerians were gunned down by the French army for having dared suggest that they, too, were awaiting their liberation.)

Rachid has no fixed address. He sleeps in a different place every night, to avoid police traps. Indeed he sleeps little, preferring to stay up all night drinking coffee and talking politics. Rachid doesn't laugh often, but when he does — caught off guard by András's gallows humor — his teeth are a shock of whiteness against the dark skin of his face.

It was Rachid who, having learned the importance a little French-German boy had taken on in his Hungarian friend's heart, had salvaged the rocking chair from a dump in Aubervilliers . . . and lost his temper when András had dared to thank him for it. Among brothers, thanks are unnecessary.

Yes, András has been accepted as a brother in the struggle.

"This is a slash," he says, meaning a stash, and Saffie frowns uncomprehendingly. So András goes on to explain. Once a month, Rachid makes the rounds of Barbès and assembles the funds collected by the *moussebilates,* then hides them here overnight. Weapons, too, on occasion. In other words, András's very first joke, the one about the bomb in the baby carriage, was scarcely a joke at all.

"You mean . . . you help to make war?" says Saffie, backing away from him. "You mean . . . these hands, they touch clarinets . . . and guns? *These hands . . . are for killing people?* I hate you!"

"Saffie . . ."

"Don't touch me! *I hate war!* András!" (She's screaming now. Genuinely hysterical this time.) "*I denounce you to the police!*"

He slaps her. As hard as he can. Just once. Just to calm her down.

And, yes, it does calm her down. . . . She brings both hands up to her face and presses them gently to her flaming cheek.

Dumbfounded by this outburst of violence between the two people he loves most in the world, Emil drops his squash flute on the floor and looks back and forth from one to the other, wide-eyed, not crying.

The truth — which both of them sense though they refrain from uttering it out loud — is that they've finally touched on the essence of their love, its secret sacred core.

What each loves in the other is the enemy.

They have now gone safely beyond the turning point.

When Raphael gets back to Paris two days later, bearing an expensive cuckoo clock as a gift for Emil, he finds Saffie more serene and radiant than ever, and it warms his heart.

That evening, as they're brushing their teeth and undressing, going through the automatic gestures of getting ready for bed, Saffie asks Raphael,

"So . . . did your concerts go well?"

"Oh yes, very well. . . . I was able to breathe. . . . Not the least remaining trace of that vicious flu, thanks to you. . . . But a problem did come up on Wednesday night. . . ."

"Ah?"

"Yes — we were playing the Mozart concerto, you know, the one with the flute duet. . . . I was facing Mathieu as usual, and for some reason, right in the middle of our solo, we looked at each other and both of us got the urge to laugh. It was dreadful! Can you imagine? You're on the verge of dissolving into laughter — but you have to control it somehow or you'll ruin the music! For a pianist or a cellist it wouldn't be so serious, but for a flutist! Sheer torture. . . . Mathieu turned red as a beet and started shaking from head to foot — his eyes were laughing, the corners of his mouth were laughing — and of course every time I looked at him I came closer to cracking up. I kept trying to concentrate on something else but it was no use; no matter what came to mind, everything seemed perfectly hilarious. . . . So you know what I finally did?"

"No?" says Saffie, neatly folding each piece of clothing as she takes it off and hanging it over the back of a chair.

"Well, I turned my back on him."

"Ah!" says Saffie. Naked, she walks over to the bed and draws her nightgown from under the pillow.

"Pretty smart, eh? The audience probably found it a bit strange, but at least we were able to make it through to the end of the piece. . . . I swear, though, for a moment there I really thought I'd have to break off playing. . . . What a disaster that would have been, can you imagine? With the concert broadcast live!"

"I'm so proud of you," murmurs Saffie absentmindedly, slipping into her nightgown.

"Yes, well, I have to admit I was pretty proud of myself. . . ."

His voice alters suddenly, descending into the deeper registers of desire.

"Come here, you. . . ." he says.

Taking his wife by the hand, he draws her to him and gazes deeply into the opaque green ponds of her eyes.

"You're very beautiful these days, you know that? You seem to be getting more and more beautiful all the time. . . ."

Setting both hands on her shoulders, visible through the transparent pearl-gray silk of her nightgown, he draws her closer still.

"You see," he says, brimming with happiness as he feels his member rise and harden against Saffie's stomach, "all I did was turn around, like this. . . ."

Turning her around, he pulls her nightgown up to her naked hips and pushes her gently forward onto the bed.

"And that way," he says, panting now, bending over her to nibble at her neck even as he begins to enter her, "I was able to . . . keep . . . going . . . yes . . . keep going . . . yes . . . yes. . . ."

Doesn't Saffie ever feel guilty? How can she go on leading a double life like this, day after day, month after month? After all, she only has one body — is there never any interference in her mind?

No. For the simple reason that she loves András, whereas she's never loved Raphael.

But doesn't the constant lying bother her conscience?

No.

Not even on the day she pronounced her wedding vows?

No. Because the ceremony took place in French, and speaking a foreign language is always a little bit like play-acting.

But then . . . with András?

Oh, that's different. When two people in love can only talk to each other in a language foreign to both, it's . . . how shall I put it? Well, no . . . I'm sorry, if you've never experienced it, I'm afraid there's no way I can explain it to you.

XIII

Ever since she told András the story of the badly buried animals — and succeeded in making him understand why lullabys stick in her throat — Saffie has grown more attentive to her son. Day by day, she's learning to see, hear and feel the tiny human being who lives by her side.

And Emil worships her. He stretches his arms up to her — "Up, Mama! *Up* in your arms!" When she picks him up, he locks his skinny legs around her waist, pats her on both cheeks, strokes her hair, wets her lips with his slobbery kisses. . . . And Saffie, at long last, dares. Her eyes pressed shut, she clasps his little body to her. Buries her nose in his silky black curls and breathes in their fragrance. Plants a tender, lingering kiss on the nape of his neck. Whispers into his ear — "my baby," "my darling," and sometimes even, very softly, "mein Schatz." Yes. She dares.

Emil keeps her company in the apartment on the Rue de Seine. He follows her from one room to another as she goes about her household chores, zigzagging around her, babbling, asking a thousand questions. His vocabulary expands dizzyingly from one day to the next.

"What's that?"

"A vacuum cleaner."

"Va . . . keaner."

"Vacuum cleaner."

"Va . . . cuum . . . keaner."

"What's that?"

"A . . ."

Saffie racks her brains for the word in French. Sometimes she can't come up with it. This time she does.

"A pitcher."

"Pisher."

"Pitch-tch-tcher."

"Pitcher."

"Good for you!"

So many tiny victories in the struggle against ignorance, vagueness, the hostile silence of the world.

"*Didi! Didi!*" cries Emil excitedly, every time a sparrow alights on the windowsill. He chose the word "Didi" a long time ago to mean bird. Saffie first says "Yes," then corrects him, carefully articulating the French word with all its vowels, oi-seau — never Vogel — never the bird of her childhood — *Kommt ein Vogel geflogen,* the one that flies up to you with a letter in its beak, *von der Mutter einen Brief* — no, that bird has been obliterated once and for all.

There's one bird they both despise — the one that pops out of the cuckoo clock Raphael brought back from Switzerland, twenty-four times a day. They're exasperated by the mechanism's ultra-Swiss accuracy — it neither loses nor gains as much as a second per month; its *ticks* and its *tocks* are relentless, imperturbable, maddening. On the quarter hour it says *ding,* on the half hour *ding dong,* at three quarters, *ding dong ding* — and then, smack on the hour, you hear with a sinking heart the spring go *thrum,* the tiny painted door fly open and the tiny painted bird pop out to open its tiny painted beak and stupidly recite, *"Cuckoo! Cuckoo!"* — up to twelve times in a row!

As Raphael can tolerate no noise of any kind when he's practicing the flute, the clock has been hung as far away as possible from his music room, namely, in the child's bedroom. When it goes off in the middle of the night, Emil often wakes up and cries.

It's unbearable.

So, the next time her husband is out of town for professional reasons, Saffie takes down the clock, carries it into the kitchen and sets it on the table.

"Come here, Emil," she says. "Now, look. . . . Where does the cuckoo live?"

"Right there. In his house."

"Yes. . . . Okay. . . . So now, we're going to open the door. . . . You see?"

She takes a pair of ice tongs and extracts the bird like a rotten tooth.

"Hooray!" cries Emil in delight.

"He's not nice, is he?"

"No. Bad cuckoo."

"You know what mama cuckoos do?"

"No . . ."

"They lay their eggs in other birds' nests, and then they just fly away. They don't want to look after their babies."

"Oh! That's *not* nice!"

"So what should we do to punish this one?"

"Let's hit it!"

"Yes! Let's hit it! Here, take this," she says, handing him the wooden mallet she uses for crushing garlic. "Go on, hit it! Good for you, Emil! Now it won't be able to wake us up anymore at night, will it?"

Laughing uproariously, they demolish the entire clock, piece by piece.

The cuckoo may be dead, and the clock on András's wall may be wildly inaccurate, but this doesn't prevent time from passing. It glides over the lovers and everyone else, in Paris and throughout the world. The new year dawns. It's called 1960, and feels heavy with menace right from the start. It marks the beginning of a new decade as well: before long, the proud symbols of the fifties — Brylcreem, Formica, nylon — will come to seem tacky and ridiculous.

What's the world up to in January of 1960? John Fitzgerald Kennedy is seeking the Democratic nomination for the next presidential election. Soloth Sar, alias Pol Pot, having picked up a certain number of theories in the course of his studies at the Sorbonne, returns to Phnom Penh to put them into practice. Vassilii Grossman is putting the finishing touches on his great novel *Life and Fate,* not suspecting that the KGB is about to raid his office, confiscating everything from the manuscript to the typewriter ribbon; he'll die believing the novel to have been destroyed. As for Albert Camus, he's working on a novel about his childhood in Algeria, not suspecting that it will remain unfinished because his life is about to come to an abrupt end on a road in Burgundy, not far from the home of Hortense Trala-Lepage. Nikita Khrushchev is thumping his fist on the table and bragging about his new nuclear bomb, a thousand times more powerful than the ones dropped on Hiroshima and Nagasaki. . . .

In Algeria, too, the days and months go by. In the steadily scorching sun or under torrential downpours, populations are displaced in the name of France, mechtas burned to the ground, bodies scientifically destroyed, corpses exposed in public to serve as a warning. The war is entering its sixth year. Little by little, hatred solidifies in souls, rage wreaks havoc in brains, hearts harden, wills steel themselves, allegiances are built, groups of fellaghas form, proliferate and arm themselves to the hilt. . . .

One day toward the end of January, outraged by what they see as Charles de Gaulle's betrayal, a group of French army generals foment yet another insurrection in Algiers — riots, state of siege, city streets littered with the bodies of the dead and dying. The insurrection is suppressed — but not before it has had time to give birth to the "Secret Army Organization" or OAS — an illegal and murderous machine designed to keep Algeria French no matter what the cost.

Meanwhile, in the northern city that is home to our protagonists, all is drizzle and drip.

András, who has been following events closely, grinds his teeth more and more frequently. He also clenches his fists — and, clenching them, feels he now has the strength to take the life of another human being.

Raphael, at this time, is at the peak of his fame. Success has done wonders for him; it inspires him; it's turning him into a genius. Now, when he plays the flute in public, both he and the flute cease to exist. All his efforts and exercises melt away, key signatures and tempi evaporate, notes detach themselves from their names, even the composer and his century become irrelevant — for what's being conveyed is of an utterly different nature, music doesn't convey music, the great musician breaks free of the particular phenomenon and rises to the atemporal level of the sublime; his fingers and lips, tongue and glottis, lungs and diaphragm have no choice but to cooperate — yes, for this Bach "Siciliana" is a pure essence, a trance beyond time and space, a divine substance in which Raphael himself is submerged at the same time as his audience. Success has become his natural milieu, the very air he draws into his lungs and breathes into his instrument. He sows the notes in the passive, fertile soil of the audience like so many magic seeds, then feels them start to germinate and blossom, finally bearing fruit in the listeners' constricted hearts, providing nourishment, appeasement, meaning. There are the honors afterward, of course

— ovations and rave reviews, flowers and money, medals and honorary degrees . . . but these are not the drug to which Raphael is addicted. His drug is the light in his listeners' eyes — an ardent, pulsating light that says: Thank you for taking us *there!* The light has become part of the cycle. Raphael needs it in order to play, and he plays in order to elicit it. The more people love him, the better he performs. The more he gives them, the greater is his gift.

It's too soon to tell whether or not Emil has inherited his father's musical talent, but he does have his breathing power. At the end of January, he blows out the two candles on his birthday cake with a single puff, and Saffie claps her hands for joy.

How can so many worlds exist simultaneously on one little planet? Which of them is the most genuine, the most precious, the most urgent for us to understand? The connections among them are complex, yet not chaotic — all of them are moving forward at the same time, rotating on their axes, colliding and colluding with one another, causes sparking off effects that become causes in turn and set off effects of their own, and so on and so forth, ad infinitum. . . .

A rather disastrous infinitum on the whole, it must be said.

At spring's end, the great Rampal invites Raphael to help him set up the International Summer Academy in Nice, destined to become one of the most prestigious flute schools in the world.

And Saffie, before going south to join her husband in the elegant house he's rented for them in Saint Tropez, explores Paris with her son and lover at greater length and with greater freedom than ever before.

The Bois de Vincennes, on a Sunday toward the end of June. The three of them are playing hide-and-seek — running, laughing, yelling, sweating, panting, Emil overjoyed to have Apu and Mama all to himself, not in conversation with each other — after which, they decide to go on a hike through the forest. The baby carriage is a thing of the past: the Prince de Sicile now walks on his own two legs — or, at most, allows himself to be carried on Apu's shoulders.

On a narrow pathway they encounter a French family — father, mother, adolescent son and chubby little daughter, also on a Sunday outing. The air around them crackles with resentment, like a cloud of static electricity. "Julien! Let the lady past!" "For heaven's sake, François! Hang onto the dog, it'll scare the little boy!" "Come over here, Suzanne, you're in the way!" "How am I supposed to get over there? There are nettles all over the place!" "Say excuse me when you walk in front of people!" "Look, now my shoes are all muddy! And it's your fault!" "Don't talk to your sister that way!"

When the cloud has passed, Saffie and András turn to one another, laughing, and kiss. Emil laughs, too — without really knowing why, just to be included in their pleasure.

Late in the afternoon, as they're in the metro on their way back to Paris, Emil surrenders to exhaustion on his mother's lap. The arm he'd twined around her neck slips down and falls heavily to his side. A sigh escapes his lips and his head tilts backward, revealing the tender lustrous skin of his neck.

The woman sitting across from them leans forward and peers through her tortoiseshell glasses at the sleeping child.

"He's so cute!" she murmurs to Saffie with a simpering smile, counting on the masochistic solidarity of mothers. "They're all adorable at that age, aren't they?"

"No," says Saffie, calmly and gravely. "You're wrong, Madam. This child is a half-Boche, a baby Nazi. He's already started to kill birds."

Crimson with indignation, the woman gets up and changes seats.

"Why do you say this?" asks András with a grin.

"Oh, it's too easy to be nice to children. 'He's so cute, he's so adorable. . . .' Why doesn't she say that *you're* adorable? Or me? Don't we deserve her kind attention? Or . . . or him, over there?" she adds, nodding in the direction of a wizened old Muslim, dressed in turban and djellaba, huddled sound asleep in one corner of the car.

"Saffie!" exclaims András in mock astonishment. "Don't tell me you're starting to see the people around you!"

Mid-July, a hot and sultry day's end, soup-yellow air. Wandering through the narrow streets of Charonne, a quarter they've never visited before, they stumble on the Place Saint Blaise. And there, on the terrace of a shoddy-looking café, two musicians have struck up a waltz. Ah yes, they'd forgotten — it's Bastille Day. Within a few hours — popular dances, rockets, firecrackers, fireworks — the whole city will be rocking with festivity.

Saffie contemplates the scene. An unspeakably banal scene — the simple pleasures of lower-class Paris. The musicians, a trumpeter and an accordionist, are past middle age and shabbily dressed . . . yet they play, and before long people begin to dance in the street: a few couples in their forties, some women with women, a handful of listless teenagers stupidly mimicking their elders.

Suddenly, Saffie is overcome with fatigue — and it has nothing to do with their long walk in the July sun — no, her fatigue is ancient and irrefutable. She wavers on her feet. Puts her hands on her son's shoulders to steady herself. Pressed up against her legs, Emil is observing the scene, too. He doesn't leap to join the other children, who are playing marbles and jacks in the gutter.

Saffie is crushed, stifled, petrified by the . . . how to put it . . . the unbearable tenuousness of the moment. She senses that all it would take is a gust of wind — a mote of dust in someone's eye — a foot stepped on by another foot — for everyone to give up and stalk away in disgust, muttering imprecations and spitting on the ground. Hate, hate and despair . . . Gradually, she feels her body being invaded by a wave of molten lead. Yes, the old layer of Blei has come to swathe her every organ and these are the wheezy Strauss waltzes revived, the old men playing as best they can and the women dancing with other women, she's dead again, and none of her new life is real, there's no such thing as Paris, or summertime, no such thing as Raphael or András or Emil. . . .

Can Emil tell that his mother is dead, from the way her fingernails are slowly sinking into his shoulders?

Dizzy with inexistence, she clutches at András's arm — and he, misunderstanding, sets Emil down in a chair on the café terrace — turns to his lover — takes her in his arms and begins to waltz with her — naturally, romantically — breathing cool air onto her burning forehead. . . . Ah! Thanks to András, the hideous unreality of the world has been held at bay once again; movement has turned back into true movement, instead of immobility in disguise; stiff legs limber up and espouse the simple rhythms of the waltz — *oom*-pah-pah, *oom*-pah-pah — the instants leap to their feet and return to take their places in reality, the event prances and capers, declaring it has the right to happen and that nothing can stop it now, couples continue to whirl and spin as the music advances, its three beats following each other calmly and predictably, not disintegrating. . . . Oh! With András's arms around her waist, Saffie could dance until the end of the world!

When the waltz is over, wet with sweat, eyes aglitter, she drops into a chair next to Emil. András orders drinks for them all — beer, ginger ale, apple juice, an extravagant expense — and they sit there until dark, watching the musicians play and the dancers dance.

"Why are the people dancing?" asks Emil.

"To celebrate the Revolution!" answers András.

"What's a Revo . . . tion?"

"It's when people get their heads cut off," says Saffie.

"So if they get their heads cut off, why are they dancing?"

The next morning, Charles de Gaulle reviews the spectacular military parade on the Champs Elysées. Five hundred aircraft thunder deafeningly overhead, including Mystère, Super Sabre, Vautour, an impressive array of new jets. Paratroopers in red berets and harkis rigged out in camouflage gear go marching down the avenue, eliciting deafening cheers from the crowd.

In the cities of Paris, Lyons, and Dijon, in the course of this same summer of 1960, Charles de Gaulle will allow eight National Liberation Front fighters to be beheaded by the guillotine.

Saffie spends the whole month of August at the house in Saint Tropez. Plays with Emil in the Mediterranean. Screams with laughter when he splashes her. Patiently helps him mold turrets for his sand castles. . . . No, she isn't rediscovering the delights of childhood — this *is* her childhood, the first time she's ever felt carefree. She sleeps like a child as well, dreaming of András almost every night. Raphael works in Nice during the week, and rushes to be with his little family when the weekend rolls around. He's thrilled to see Saffie looking so tanned and fit.

"You're simply glowing," he tells her.

How could it be otherwise?

Her sense of well-being lasts until the autumn.

But at the end of November, insomnia — with its familiar procession of ghosts — returns to plague her. One day, in András's workshop, she feels just awful.

Unable to continue reading, she slips behind the red blanket and goes to lie down on the couch. Crooks her right arm over her eyes to shield them from the light. András comes to join her, after having set Emil up at the workbench with a piece of cardboard and bits of cork to glue onto it.

As on the day when he told her about the mark of the angel, he takes her head on his lap and traces her features with his blunt yet agile fingertips.

"What's this?" he asks, smoothing two deep creases of tension between Saffie's eyebrows with his index finger.

"It's the mark of my father," says Saffie.

The words have escaped from her lips. She's aghast. How can she have said such a thing? Now she'll have to explain. András is waiting. So she continues, blurting out the first thing that comes into her head.

"It's because my father worked for Bayer during the war, so when I have a headache I always think of him. . . ."

At once, András knows she's lying. He has a sixth sense where lies are concerned. He has no idea which part of her sentence contains the serpent. Knows only that he's hurtling away from Saffie right now, like a meteorite plummeting through space. Has no wish to interrogate her.

"Bayer?" he repeats in an empty voice, latching arbitrarily onto the proper noun.

"Yes . . . you know, the big chemical complex in Leverkusen. . . . Because he's interested in . . . you know . . . anesthesia? For killing pain . . . a friend gets him a job with Bayer, so he doesn't do his military service. I mean, this is his military service — instead of going to fight on the Eastern Front — because of his ear that doesn't hear."

Saffie is floundering, fleeing — András can scarcely hear what she's saying anymore; all he can hear is the sound of her flight.

". . . That's why, in the winter of '45, we can't go away. You understand? The Russians keep getting closer and closer, everybody is leaving the area, thousands of . . . Flüchtlinge, people running away in the cold and the snow, by train, by sleigh, by foot, with nothing, no food, nothing — little children and old people dropping dead at the side of the road, horses dropping dead, mothers giving birth in the snow with their children watching, everyone keeps running from here to there and then from there to here. . . ." (András knows all this, and Saffie knows he knows it; what's she telling it to him for?) ". . . But not us. We have to stay in our house, because my father is alive, he's going to come home — and if we leave, how will he find us? So we stay where we are, we wait and wait . . . and then at last . . . in September, he comes home."

András clenches his jaws and leaves the room. Returns, a while later, with a cup of herbal tea and honey.

"Try to rest," he tells her. "The sun is out, I take a walk with Emil. We go play on the sand mountains by the Seine. Try to sleep, Saffie."

The tall blond man and the small dark boy run hand in hand along the embankments of the Seine. Then András hikes Emil up onto his shoulders and bounces him along, humming, making up a song —

> *My papa*
> *is a bourgeois*
> *My grandma*
> *is a landowner*
> *And me? And me? And me?*

"I like can-dee!" cries Emil, shrieking with laughter, and they start again. The child is not yet three.

> *My papa? A big fat bourgeois!*
> *My grandma? A filthy landowner!*
> *And me? I love can-dee!*

They invent other variations, toiling up the steep hills of sand and whooshing down them on flattened cardboard boxes.

Later that afternoon, as they're walking home, Emil repeats the rhyme to his mother. Saffie puts a hand over her mouth and titters, half shocked and half amused. Warns him never to sing it in front of his father. Hugs him to her side as they walk.

"Up you go, sweetheart!"

Emil can now climb up the steps to the Pont des Arts by himself, even if it is on all fours.

"Look," says Saffie, taking the stuffed poodle leg from her bag. "Do you think it can float?"

"Yeah!" says the child.

"Who gets to throw it in — you or me?"

"Me!"

"Okay. . . . On your mark, get set, go!"

The leg plummets down in a straight line, slips without a splash beneath the oily green waters of the Seine, and bobs back up to the surface.

"It can foat, Mama! It can foat!"

"Terrific! Let's say good-bye to the poodle leg, okay?"

"Bye, poo-deg! Bye!"

"And have a good trip!"

"Have a good trip, poo-deg!"

XIV

In December 1960, after having announced his intention to hold a referendum on the Algerian situation the following month, Charles de Gaulle flies to Algeria for what he is certain will be a triumphal visit. But the pieds noirs, enraged at the prospect of losing the land their ancestors had stolen, demonstrate against him in one city after another. They riot in Algiers and set upon the Muslims; the Muslims demonstrate in protest and clash violently with French soldiers; things degenerate so quickly that the president is forced to cut his visit short.

Ah, yes, there's no doubt about it — things are falling apart. The situation will get worse before it gets better, before it gets worse again, and so on and so forth.

The Prince of Sicily celebrates his third birthday.

At last, Saffie and András decide he's too old to remain in the next room while they make love. So he goes outside to play in the courtyard while Mama and Apuka are busy behind the red blanket. He has so many friends in the building that he's never alone for long.

One day, though, he discovers that he also has enemies. It's Saturday morning, and he's helping Madame Blumenthal trudge up the one hundred and nineteen steps with her shopping bags, when a group of teenage boys in kippas, fresh from synagogue, start pounding up the stairs behind them. As they pass in a thundering of feet and a jostling of bodies, they mutter into Emil's ear, "Boche, Boche, filthy Boche, asshole Nazi, son-of-a-bitch . . ."

Emil doesn't understand.

He asks his mother about it later, as they're walking home.

"What's a Boche?"

"Someone called you a Boche?"

"Yes."

"Oh, don't pay any attention, Schatz. Only stupid people talk like this. They think you're nice if you come from their country, and not nice if you come from somewhere else. Isn't that stupid?"

"But Apu does it, too."

"What do you mean?"

"He calls Papa a bourgeois."

Saffie titters.

"Oh, but that's different!" she says. "Bourgeois isn't a country! Anyway, András is just joking when he says that. He knows your papa is a fine man."

"I like Apu better."

"Yes, I know. So do I. . . ."

"What does landowner mean?"

"Oh, that!" says Saffie, laughing outright. "You shouldn't make fun of your grandma, you've never even met her!"

"But what does it mean?"

"Nothing. . . . It's the same thing as bourgeois — it's when you've got lots of money and and you don't want to share it with the poor."

"That's mean!"

"Hey, let's run, my feet are freezing! I race you to the next lamppost!"

In Paris, virtually every night of the year 1961, police burst into cafés and hotels frequented by Algerians and shove them down into the basement or out into the street at the point of their submachine guns — even in their pajamas, even in midwinter. The ones they decide to arrest are hauled either to the local police station or out to a barracks beyond the city limits, where harkis take over. The chief of police has set up a special auxiliary force comprised exclusively of harkis because, in addition to beating the men to a pulp, they can insult them in Arabic — to ensure that their souls suffer as much damage as their bodies.

When the Algerians of Paris are not being harassed by harkis, they're being harassed by FLN militants. Rachid harasses them, for instance. His job is to make the rounds of the *moussebilates* once a month and pick up the dues they've collected. It's for the War of Liberation, it's compulsory, you don't have a choice, you give, period, no questions asked. Four hundred thousand Algerian workers pay their dues every month, contributing an annual total of over five billion francs to the cause ("old francs," since last year's devaluation). Factory workers are required to pay Fr 3500 a month, plus a "gift" of 500. Prostitutes pay varying amounts, depending on the neighborhood. In Barbès they have to hand over thirty thousand; in Pigalle, sixty; in the Place Clichy, eighty; on the Champs Elysées, a hundred. Money from the Champs is particularly satisfying. It gets extracted from the wallet of a wealthy Frenchman and begins to circulate, moving from the whore to the *moussebilate* and from the *moussebilate* to Rachid, who stuffs it along with thousands of other banknotes into a battered old suitcase, then hides the suitcase at András's place overnight; early the next morning ardent young French Leftists pick it up and carry it home with them, then take out the money, count it carefully, pin it into wads and hand it over to Monsieur C., who stacks it in Dior hatboxes and conveys it to the Paris branch of a large Swiss bank, where an agent transfers it by telex to Geneva — where, thanks to the accommodating attitude of a Swiss banker who happens to be a former Nazi, Madame C. withdraws it and hands it over to FLN militants who are hiding out in a four-star hotel disguised as Sudanese emirs and who, after downing a few bottles of champagne so as to avert possible suspicion, transform what's left of the money into machine guns that will be used to blow out the brains of Frenchmen in Algeria. Pure pleasure, I tell you. . . .

In June 1961, in the basement of a Paris police station, two infuriated police officers take Rachid's fine brown hands and smash them with a hammer, breaking each of his fingers joint by joint. Then they let him go. . . .

His hands will be of no further use to him. They'll no longer be able to carry suitcases. They'll never hold a scalpel.

The mutilation has just happened when Saffie sees Rachid for the second time. It's Midsummer's Eve; Raphael has already left for Nice. The Paris sky is blue-mauve streaked with pink, the air is tepid and fragrant — and Bill, the tenor sax player, has invited some friends of his to jam in the instrument maker's courtyard. As the group lacks a percussionist, András has given Emil a couple of wooden spoons and asked him to bang on the metal garbage can. Drawn by the weird racket, people in the street — prostitutes from n° 34, bloated dinner clients from Goldenberg's delicatessen, bored teenagers — stick their heads through the porte cochère, then walk all the way in; even Madame Blumenthal, up on the seventh floor, throws her windows open wide to listen.

Rachid is crouching alone in a darkened corner of the courtyard. His hands, wrapped in white bandages, dangle uselessly between his thighs. Recognizing him, Saffie sets down the tray of tea glasses she was passing around and bends over to speak to him.

"Are you thirsty?" she whispers, with a gesture to show she's willing to hold the glass to his lips.

"Thank you," acquiesces Rachid, looking away.

And so, crouching down in turn, the German woman holds a glass to the Algerian's lips in the courtyard of the Hungarian, amid the syncopated jazz riffs of the African-Americans.

. . . .

The summer is stifling. Violence proliferates, both in Algeria and in metropolitan France. Tit for tat and tat for tit — the cycle of attacks and reprisals intensifies, seems as if it will never stop. Bing! A policeman murdered by a Muslim. Bang! Three Muslims gunned down by policemen. Bong! OAS. Bang bang! FLN. Atrocities and counteratrocities. Policemen's wives in tears, soldiers' mothers in tears, Hortense Trala-Lepage in tears (since the January referendum, she's had to face the fact that the days of her Algerian vineyards may be numbered), assassinations and mutilations, people running for their lives, bullets ripping through stomachs and brains, faces smashed in, throats slit, Arab women ceaselessly ululating, Arab children squealing in terror, crops ruined, villages razed, the bodies of young white and brown men humiliated, dismembered, murdered, buried, mourned — the old, old story we persist in calling "the news."

. . . . . .

Meanwhile, Saffie cavorts with Emil in the turquoise waters of the Mediterranean, allows the sun to brown her white skin, drowses in the shade of the palm trees.

One evening at dinner, as he's serving up the mullet with tomatoes and green peppers that Saffie has cooked, Raphael says to Emil,

"Well, my boy! You're getting pretty big, aren't you?"

"Yes, Papa," replies Emil, smiling tolerantly. He hates it when adults address him in an adult-addressing-a-child tone of voice.

"Isn't it about time you started school?"

Saffie upsets the glass of white wine she's just lowered from her lips, spilling it on the tablecloth.

"School?" she says, so taken aback she doesn't even rise to get the sponge. "But he's far too young!"

"Not at all!" says Raphael with a grin. "I don't know what the system's like in Germany, but in France the government pays for children's schooling as of age three. And how old are you, young man?"

"Three and a half," replies Emil stiffly, annoyed at having to recite facts well known to all.

"Three and a half! My goodness! You *are* just about a young man!" Raphael ruffles Emil's mass of black curls, and it's all the boy can do not to wrench himself away from his father's touch. "It's high time your little rump met up with one of those hard wooden benches!"

"Is . . . is it necessary?" stammers Saffie, struggling to control her rising panic.

"You mean compulsory? No, not until the age of six. But seriously, I think it would be good for Emil to play with kids his own age. Especially since we won't be giving him any brothers and sisters. . . ."

He gazes tenderly at Saffie, to make sure she won't interpret this as a reproach.

"It's not good for him to spend all of his time with us old folks," he adds, carrying his fork to his mouth, "even if we *are* remarkable in every way."

Emil knows better than to challenge any part of this statement.

"But I don't want him to go to school!" Saffie bursts out, though she has no idea how she's going to answer the question Raphael will inevitably ask next.

"Why not?" says Raphael.

"Because we go for walks," suggests Emil.

"Yes, I know," says Raphael. "This mullet is perfectly scrumptious — a real treat! But as Herr Doktor Freud says, a boy can't spend his entire life going for walks with his mother. A bit of the reality principle, for heaven's sake! That's what fathers are for."

Saffie has come up with an answer, thanks to Emil's intervention.

"I can't go walking alone in Paris," she says. "You know . . . men in the streets . . . they respect mothers, but . . . Besides, it does me so much good for my health. . . . And we learn lots of things, you know . . . about the history of France . . . and . . . and trees. . . . It's even better than school!"

Grasping at straws, poor dear. She'd grasp at anything. Emil is her pretext, her alibi, the *sine qua non* of her love affair with András. Emil is their hostage. (What does she intend to do three years from now? She has no idea. For people madly in love, life is an endless series of nows, carefully propped up by a censored past and a nebulous future.)

Though puzzled, Raphael eventually gives in — convinced less by Saffie's arguments than by the fact that, for once, she has forcefully expressed a wish for something.

He'll give in again, though with greater reluctance, in the summer of '62.

And yet again — this time with genuine alarm — in the summer of '63.

Emil won't attend school.

. . . .

August rolls around, and the Lepage family return to Paris. Father locks himself away to rehearse for a historic recording session — J. S. Bach's complete *Sonatas for Flute and Harpsichord,* with the great harpsichordist Sonya Feldman.

Mother and son grab hands and run — run — run toward the Pont des Arts. The concierge stands watching them through her ground-floor window, a glass of pastis in one hand. She shakes her head and smiles. Looks as if Madame Lepage is in terrific shape — well, good for her! She herself, Mademoiselle Blanche, has had a bad case of phlebitis these past few months. Every step causes her acute pain. To distribute the morning mail, she now has to take the elevator not only up but down, one floor at a time.

. . . .

"Did you see what's going on in your city?" András asks Saffie as they are getting dressed after love, after tea, after more love.

"My city?"

Saffie has no idea what he means. They live in the same city.

"Berlin."

The word thuds into her gut like a fist, taking her breath away. She shakes her head.

"Saffie . . . You didn't hear?"

"No."

The blood has stopped circulating in her body. It descends into her toes and fingertips, where it turns into lead. *Your city — Berlin* — she doesn't speak that language.

"They build a wall to cut the city in two. Too many people are leaving the East to go into the West. More than thirty thousand, just this summer. More than two million since '49."

"A *wall?* . . ."

"Yeah. It's cutting across the whole city. With barbwire, guards, machine guns . . . lots of pretty decorations."

"No . . . don't. . . ."

András: "You always want to know nothing, Saffie? Even when it's your own country?"

"I'm French," says Saffie, stupidly, stubbornly.

"Ah yes. Right. You're French, and I am Chinese," says András, raising his left arm in a Red Guard salute. "Long live Mao Ze-dong!"

"No, you're not Chinese, you're communist," says Saffie. "But it doesn't work, your communist system! Why did you leave Hungary then, if you like communism so much? Why the people in the West don't try to go into the East? Or to the wonderful Marxist paradise you prepare for them in Algeria?"

"*Ech!*" says András, shaking his head sarcastically. "She has a great political mind, this Madame Lepage! All these years I think she doesn't read the newspapers, but in fact she teaches political science in the university! Everyone should stand up and clap for Madame Lepage!"

"You make fun when you have no answer," says Saffie, not un-justifiably. "Oh, I'm *fed up!* Always *war, war, WAR!*"

She rises to leave.

"No . . . Saffie . . . I'm sorry. I want to show you something. Come . . ."

He kisses both her hands.

Goes outside to call Emil.

An hour later, the three of them are standing on the metal bridge that spans the circular route to the west of Paris.

This time, unlike the day on which he forced Saffie to confront the Rue des Rosiers, András has no need to tell her to look. She's looking.

What's sprawled on the far side of the circular route, brown and gray and black as far as the eye can see, is neither Bombay nor São Paolo — it's Nanterre, one of the inner suburbs of the City of Light. Virtually one hundred percent Muslim. Tin roofs, held in place with stones or plastic washtubs. Breeze-block walls. Skeletons of trucks and subway cars salvaged from scrap heaps. Wrecked automobiles. Stray dogs. Scattered rubbish. Mud everywhere. Clothes dangling from makeshift clotheslines. Filthy puddles, crawling with flies.

This is where the men who repair the streets of Paris return in the evening to eat and sleep. Most but not all of them have left their wives and children in Algeria. Some actually house their families in this jumble of hutches and hovels, crumbling shacks, cement sheds, broken brick cubicles. They live on top of each other, crowded six or seven to a room (not counting the rats) and two or three to a bed. Two hundred and fifty families draw their water from the same pump.

The scene shimmers and quivers in the burning light of the sun, like a mirage in the Sahara Desert. Saffie stares at it, shading her eyes with one hand. And András, staring at her staring at it, senses that something is about to happen.

"Emil," he says, leading the boy a little way along the bridge. "You know a good game? You pick up stones and then you throw them down on the cars below."

"Can I, Mama?" asks Emil incredulously.

"Of course you can Mama," says András. "But only one at a time, okay? And later, you come and tell us how many cars you killed."

"Okay!"

"No cheating, hey?"

"Yeah . . . uh . . . no!"

András returns to Saffie's side and waits. Now she's got to say something. Now she's got to be the one to say something.

"You have to understand, András," she says at last. "The wall in Berlin, it doesn't change anything. We Germans, we all live with a wall in our heads. Ever since the war . . . and even before. . . . For me, all my life. A wall between . . . what we can say . . . and what we can't. . . . The questions we can ask . . . and the others."

András remains silent. How often has he remained silent now, listening to Saffie? How often has he deemed it preferable to hold his tongue — to protect her, because she's so young and vulnerable? And even here, even today, confronted with the ig-nominious poverty of the Algerians, all she can think of is her own suffering. . . .

"My father, in Tegel in '46 — my mother is already dead — they hold a Spruchkammer to judge him. You know. The court to see if you were a Nazi. It's all over very soon. In two hours, he's . . . unbelastet. They say he was only a . . . a Mitläufer, that he ran along beside the others."

I must be dreaming, thinks András. He's always known. Since the day he first set eyes on her, he's known that Saffie's father was a Nazi, a criminal, a monster; that he took an active part in the abomination. He has no wish to learn the details of the paternal sins weighing on her conscience — always *her* conscience! He's on the verge of interrupting her, lashing out at her, when he notices the change in her voice.

Saffie's lovely deep husky voice has given way to a voice he's never heard before. Lifeless, bloodless, strangely disincarnate — yes, this new voice of hers is almost a thing, almost an object in the world, as metallic and indifferent as the bridge on which they're standing. . . . Moreover, it no longer seems to be addressing him.

"My older brother, the one in the Hitlerjugend, little by little he goes insane. In '53, they lock him up in a . . . an Asyl. And the next year, Frau Silber goes to Köln to live with her sister. So I'm the oldest child, and when my father has an attack in '55, I'm the one to look after everything. I'm eighteen, it's my last year at the Gymnasium, the doctors tell me he will die — perhaps in a month, perhaps in a year, but I should put his papers in order. Vati can't walk anymore, he can't talk — but he's *there,* completely there, his eyes are protesting as if to explode, it makes him furious to know he will die, he's only fifty years old. I look after him just like Emil, I dress him and undress him, feed him and clean him. . . . Also I read him the newspaper, and go through his files. Alles ist in Ordnung."

I know what comes next, thinks András. I know it by heart. This is where, rummaging through her father's papers, the young woman comes across his SA membership card, and the record book proving that the family is Aryan to the third generation. "What on earth!" she says to herself, stunned. "No! Impossible! My wonderful Vati who loved animals so much? I can't believe it!" Etcetera.

But Saffie's robotlike voice veers off in an unexpected direction.

"One morning I go down for the mail and there's a letter from Monsieur Ferrat, my French teacher from before. He's gone back to France, to Lyons, and now he sends me this letter. Or rather, five letters. Not from him. From Bayer. He knows my father was in Leverkusen. The letters have been published in France, in a newspaper, and he sends me that, just the page of the newspaper in French, with the letters from Bayer to Auschwitz. I know them by heart. The experiments with sleeping pills. The order for one hundred and fifty women. The haggling over the price. The deal finally concluded. Thank you, we have received the shipment. The women are a bit skinny but we accept them. The experiment has been carried out. It was successful, thank you. All the women are dead. Soon we will contact you for another shipment."

Saffie's voice peters out. The only sound is the incessant, nerve-wracking hum of the cars on the road below as they approach, roar past, and recede into the distance. . . . András has closed his eyes. His hands grip the bridge railing as if to break it. Every time he thinks he's learned the worst, heard all there is to hear, someone comes along with a new horror story. For as long as he lives, there will always be a story he's never heard before. It's unending, literally inexhaustible — what a godsend for novelists, that Hitler!

"I finish reading that," Saffie stubbornly pursues, "and . . . I don't know. I don't know anything. I go upstairs to my father. He's in his armchair. I hold the paper in front of his eyes — he has green eyes like mine, still perfect vision — I see him read, then stop reading, and I say, Well? Did you know? Did you hear about this? Sleeping pills — that's your department, isn't it? Did they tell you about these experiments?"

Not once, as she speaks, does Saffie avert her gaze from the vile panorama of the Nanterre slums. Not once does her voice deviate from its monotonous gray metallic line of notes.

"*Did you know?* I scream at him. I go up to his right ear and read the letters out loud to him, screaming. I take him by the shoulders, I shake him, I hit him. He's . . . like a statue. Heavy and stiff. A block of refusal. Even his eyes stop moving now. And in the evening, he's dead."

. . . . . .

Did Saffie really scream into her father's ear that day? She can't quite remember for sure. She *thinks* she must have screamed at him — or at least read the letters out loud to him in a firm, clear voice — but she isn't sure. She can't be sure anymore.

"*Four!*" cries Emil running back toward them along the bridge, his face ablaze with joy. "I killed *four* cars, Apu!"

"Four, you killed," mutters András, exhausted. "Yeah, but what color? I forgot to tell you — red cars bring more points than blue ones."

Yes. He chooses to remain silent yet again.

As they're heading back to Paris in the bus, he puts an arm around Saffie's rigid shoulders and whispers into her ear,

"So even the Germans, they haggle over prices? . . . That's not nice, you know. If the Germans start to haggle, what's left to us Jews?"

But Saffie doesn't laugh at his joke, and neither does he.

The next time they're together, the next time they find themselves naked in a bed, András cannot. Their bodies arch and grapple, twine and twist and sweat — but they fail to unite.

And the time after that (with Emil at a safe distance, up on the seventh floor gobbling candy, playing with Madame Blumenthal's cat and listening politely but uncomprehendingly as she tells him the sad tale of her life in Yiddish) — the time after that, from the innermost core of their embrace, which is no longer merely an interlocking of limbs but also of black memories, hatreds, losses — violence rears its head. They make love and at the same time András hits her, slowly and deliberately, with the palm of his left hand, András's hand crashes down onto Saffie's face, again and again — and Saffie puts up no struggle whatsoever, makes not the least attempt to protect herself — on the contrary, she surrenders herself to her lover unreservedly — holding back nothing, for herself or for her husband or for her son . . . indeed, there's no reason they should stop before death ensues, yes, it would be almost natural for András — squeezing Saffie's neck between his huge strong hands, the hands of a martyred child grown huge, and punishing, through her, her deaf apoplectic father and the entire deaf apoplectic German people, to say nothing of the ss, the Arrow Cross, the Catholic neighbor in Buda who once spat in his mother's face, and especially, especially, his own cowardice and his own impotence — to strangle her as he ejaculates his agonizing soul into her body. Yes, I think they could have gone that far, alone in the world on that incandescent August afternoon, fucking spastically, gasping, drenched in sweat, sliding consensually into an abyss of muteness and madness . . . but they don't.

XV

Fall arrives, bringing no reprieve from summer's scorching heat. Just as the Second World War coincided with an unprecedented series of harsh winters in Europe, now, soaring temperatures seem to reflect the ebullience of the political situation — as if, in times of extremity, the cosmos entered into a weird harmony with the puny concerns of man. Tense and torrid, the weeks of September inch by, and the coming of October brings no relief — the trees continue to cling to their leaves, more blood is shed, Parisian women stroll down the street in their summer dresses, ten Algerians bite the dust for every policeman murdered.

András and Saffie are closer than they've ever been before. Though they haven't broached anew the issue of their respective political allegiances, they behave as if every difference of opinion between them had been effaced — purged, brought to catharsis as it were, by erotic violence. Saffie feels the weight of her childhood lifted from her shoulders, as if she'd spent ten years on an analyst's couch. She's gay, tender, rejuvenated — and, what's more, attentive. At long last, she's beginning to take in the world around her — through sight, hearing, smell . . . but especially through András's words.

She listens to him.

Today, October 8, he's talking loud and fast and somewhat incoherently as he paces back and forth in his workshop. Emil, who had leaped to embrace him when they arrived — "Apuka! Edesapa!" — was unceremoniously set back down on the ground and sent out to the courtyard.

To be accurate, András isn't so much talking as he is shouting. He's saying No. He's saying that this — this — yes, that this time, France has gone too far.

"Saffie, do you know what it means, a curfew?"

Saffie does know, but suspects that her German childhood memories might not be welcome in this context.

"A curfew for Muslims. Only twenty years after the curfew for Jews. Same thing! Same thing! Except 8:30 PM for the Muslims and 8 PM for the Jews. Just so the Jew doesn't go thinking he's a Muslim. But — same thing. You know why Madame Blumenthal lives alone? Because her husband, he was buying food at 6 PM, the Jews were allowed only from four to five — and good-bye Monsieur Blumenthal! Police station, Drancy, Buchenwald, Paradise! The Muslims, they work at night, or else far away from home, they get back late, when can they buy food? And you saw Nanterre!

The only life they *have* is outside, in the café, in the street. . . . And now, if a cop sees them after 10 PM — in jail! And what's next? We accept this, and what's next?"

András is shouting, gesticulating, dripping with sweat.

"Calm down, my love. . . . You go too fast. . . ."

"*I* go too fast? Not fast enough! The French are going fast, *much* faster than me! Believe me, Saffie! Tomorrow they tell the Muslims, come down to the police station and buy your croissants."

"Your croissants? . . ."

"You know . . . the crescent moon of Islam, to wear on their arm, like the yellow star."

"No . . ."

"No — you're right, they don't need it, you can see a Muslim right away, he doesn't hide like a Jew behind a nice normal white man's face. *Saffie* . . ."

"András . . ."

"*. . . I must leave!*"

Saffie stares at an oboe reed that András has just finished trimming at his workbench. Over and over again, her eyes caress the little tongue of wood, taking in its shape, its grain, its smooth blondness . . . is it really made of reed? András explained to Emil how reeds are made, the other day, but she can't remember.

"I'm going away for a while . . . to try to help . . . Rachid and our brothers. . . ."

Closing her eyes and folding her arms across her stomach, Saffie slowly bends forward until her forehead touches her knees.

"*Listen,* Saffie. Please understand! I always say, people let the Nazis do what they want, they don't notice six million people getting killed — 'Oh, dear, what happened? My goodness! If only we knew!' — Scheisse, Saffie! Well, *I know!* I know what's going on! Already, near to Paris, there are concentration camps for Muslims!"

Saffie is rocking back and forth and moaning softly, like Frau Silber on the day she lost her daughter Lotte.

"During the Occupation, there was a couple . . . *Saffie, listen to me!*" he shouts, kneeling on the floor next to her chair. *"Stop* crossing your arms! *Stop* closing your eyes! This couple, they're good at keeping files. They give the addresses of all the Jews to the police. They do an excellent job. Four thousand Jews deported in May '41. Thirteen thousand in July '42. Deported from *here,* Saffie! The whole Marais emptied! You never ask yourself why all the dead streets, the houses with boards, the windows with bricks, the stores in ruins? *Seventeen thousand Jews,* first in this couple's address book, then in the shower! Zyklon B! After the war, the couple are arrested, they're sent to prison for life."

"But András . . . ," says Saffie in a pitiful little voice, "what about your work? How will you —"

"LISTEN TO ME!"

Grabbing her by the shoulders, he forces her to look into his eyes, where erotic and political passion are vying with each other.

"Listen. This couple — Rachid told me the story. Last year they're taken out of prison. You know why? Because the police need them to make files of the Muslims. You understand, Saffie? *It's still happening!* The people who arrest the Muslims now, they're the same Scheissköpfe that deport the Jews in '42! The French generals who torture in Algeria now, they learn their job here — with the Gestapo!"

He crouches at his mistress's feet, trembling with the effort to contain his rage. Saffie lays her head on his and lightly circles his shoulders with her arms. Just to sense the warmth and weight of the body she loves, before it moves away from her, in the direction of danger. . . .

Emil has come back into the workshop. Now he asks, very timidly, "Apu? What's the matter with Apu? . . . Is he sick? . . . Did he fall down?"

"No, no," Saffie tells him. "Apu is going away on a trip."

Emil knows all about men going away on trips.

"Will you bring me a present?" he asks.

András says nothing. Seizing the child, he crushes him to his chest and heaves one terrible sigh after another — until Emil, ill at ease, finally protests and wriggles free.

.   .   .   .   .   .

The autumn heat persists . . . and drives them apart.

How long? Saffie wanted to know — and András, of course, was unable to tell her.

They agreed that she'd come to the workshop every Wednesday morning until . . . until . . . well, until things . . . The problem is that their story never had a future. It had never occurred to them that they might need to part — and, therefore, to get in touch.

.   .   .   .   .

András is seething. Electrified with hatred. Longing to fight. Now. To get in there. Be Rachid's hands. Where things are happening. Not cut off, not hiding behind a coal pile, not preferring comfort, safety, music. It's the fray he wants now, with his body. Rage. To express the rage with his body. To serve as hands for Rachid and the others — with them, against this France. Against the politicians the policemen the paratroopers all the powerful men convinced of their white right to tread on brown throats, anywhere in the world. To be there. His body. Moving. Helping. Driving the car, with Rachid and Mohammed crouched down in the back seat — the police don't stop whites for identity checks. Parking the car at the edges of the slums. Going in with them. Going in. One foot in front of the other. András and Rachid and Mohammed, armed with metal and lead, strong not weak, strengthened by their convictions, their authority, the revolution they carry in their hearts.

The body serves a purpose, it can change the course of history. Now. We must protest now. Rise up together. Get to our feet. Rachid is András's tongue and András is Rachid's hands. On the steering wheel and in the slums. Get to your feet. Close up shop. Go on strike. All of you — now — protest. *Come, march, be.* So they won't be able to say of you, as they did of us — passive sheep, marching off willingly to the slaughter.

The brothers trust the Hungarian. They see how his jaws are clenched — as tightly as the jaws of a trap — and hear the words caught in the trap — unspoken words, like their own.

Stand up! In Arabic, the brothers explain the situation. Back home, our brothers and sisters have had so many marches and look at us — not one! Look at Rachid's hands — look at them! broken, mangled by the police, it's getting worse every day, more and more brothers are getting searched, arrested, rounded up, thrown onto cement floors in Vincennes, interrogated in police station basements, stripped to the skin, forced to sit on bottles, beaten to a pulp, tossed into the Seine. We live in fear, we're afraid all the time, in the metro, in cafés and restaurants, in the street, waking up in the morning, or in the middle of the night, with cops bursting into our houses, breaking down our doors, smashing our furniture, terrorizing our wives, tearing up our pay slips and rent receipts. . . .

And — back home in Algeria — how many brothers tortured, dismembered, massacred, dead? So many. András reads the papers. He knows the numbers, for this people as for his own — unimaginable numbers — but you've got to force yourself to imagine them — one, one, one, one — not get lazy and start thinking in thousands, tens and hundreds of thousands, no, remember — every man a child, every woman a wife or mother in mourning, every shattered brain a world extinguished like a candle — so come with us now, say the brothers, come and demonstrate, protest against the curfew! András accompanies them from one alley to the next as they explain, repeat, obtain the agreement of every man in Nanterre and Gennevilliers — yes they'll go on strike next Tuesday, yes they'll close up shop to take part in the march with their wives and children, yes they'll obey orders, follow instructions so as not to create traffic jams, yes they'll make sure it's a peaceful march, with no weapons at all — not even a nail file, not even a pebble — no shouting, no ululating. . . . A demonstration of dignity.

They're frightened at the thought of going unarmed. They're right to be frightened.

The utmost secrecy surrounds the organization of the march. It has to be a surprise. Only the elderly and the crippled are allowed to remain at home . . . and those FLN militants whose faces might be familiar to the Paris police.

.   .   .   .

The first Wednesday — the eleventh of October, just two days after András's departure — Saffie goes back to the Rue du Roi de Sicile knowing it's too soon.

Still, it's a shock.

He'd told her to use her key and spend time in the workshop with Emil if she felt like it — but it's out of the question. Deserted by the beloved presence, the workshop seems mute, frozen, rejecting. She stands there motionless in the courtyard, crushed by the heat, blinded by the dazzle of musical instruments in the window.

Come to me, Saffie! calls the abyss, holding its arms out wide to her. Warum willst du nicht kommen? Ich bin dein wirkliches Heim. . . . In meinen Armen musst du schön schlafen. . . . Come and rest in my arms, I am your one true home. The German language comes back to life in her brain and torments her, crooning the sarcastic lullabies of madness — Guten Abend, gute Nacht. . . .

"Can we buy some ice cream, Mama?"

Thank God for Emil. Her son brings her back to reality. She looks at him, overcome with gratitude. His mischievous bright eyes, his ebony corkscrew curls (Raphael says it's high time he had a haircut), the sticky little hand he slips into hers when they've finished eating their vanilla cones, purchased at Berthillon's and licked to nothingness on the Quai de Béthune in the shade of the sophora trees, kissing her with his sticky little mouth and exclaiming, just to take her mind off her troubles, "I *love* vanilla ice cream! It's almost as good as you are!"

For Emil's sake, she has to keep herself from floundering, giving in to the old vertigo, reverting to what she was before she met András — a wisp of straw tossed on a roiling black swell of fear. For Emil's sake, she must remain in the here and now — France, the month of October 1961 — and not lose her grip.

Breaking with all her habits, Saffie starts to listen to the radio. Immerses herself in "the news." Forces herself to keep up with "events." Tells herself she's closer to András this way — and that, were he here, he'd certainly approve.

. . . .

The following Wednesday, October 18, a problem arises. A big problem.

Raphael had come home late from rehearsal the preceding night, drenched to the bone and in a state of shock. Saffie, who'd been doing the ironing as she waited up for him, had had some difficulty grasping exactly what had happened. . . . He'd taken the metro at the Porte d'Orléans at seven o'clock; a light rain was falling but everything was calm; upon emerging at the Odéon intersection twenty minutes later, he'd been plunged into utter pandemonium. Sheets of rain falling from a black sky — crowds of Muslims eddying and vociferating — police lights flashing — sirens screaming — thousands of women ululating hysterically —

thunder rumbling — children wailing — windows shattering in stores and overturned cars — skulls cracking under truncheons — forks of lightning illuminating bleeding faces and wild eyes. . . .

"At one point," says Raphael, "I was so much in the thick of it that my flute was knocked out of my hands, and when I bent to pick it up I nearly got trampled by the crowd. I've never been so terrified in my life! Seriously, Saffie — for a minute there, I thought I'd breathed my last breath. . . ."

Still in a daze, white as a sheet, Raphael had taken the bath towel his wife was holding out to him and dried his forehead with it, then dropped onto the couch. He kept reliving in his mind the scene of cacophonic chaos — a torture for his ears, what with the piercing screams of women and sirens and the ceaselessly repeated slogan — *"Algeria for the Algerians! Algeria for the Algerians!"* — bodies galvanized by fear and adrenaline colliding with his own, elbows knees feet heads shoulders madly thrashing, everything moving at an insane pace — and then — the godawful emptiness in his hands, in his soul, when his Louis Lot had been knocked from his grasp and, crouching down in the fray, he'd caught sight of it in the gutter, amid gushing mud and rainwater, kicked left and right by the scuffling feet of strangers.

"You understand, Saffie," Raphael had said, speaking in a low slow voice as if in a dream, still staring straight ahead into the black pandemonium from which he'd just escaped, "music is my way of taking part in the struggle, making the world a better place to live. It's what I can do. There'll always be injustice in the world, uprisings and wars, people forced to sacrifice happiness today in the hope of making the future livable for their children. But somehow . . . happiness and beauty . . . still have to be *embodied in the here and now*. It's a political act to make this possible in the real world. It's almost a political *duty* for people like me, who've had all sorts of gifts and privileges since birth — money, health, talent. . . . So . . . when I thought I'd lost my flute in the confusion . . . you know? . . . It was as if . . . as if I'd lost everything, the very meaning of . . ."

Could Saffie be moved by this speech?

She didn't hear a word it. She wasn't listening to Raphael. Seated next to him on the couch, she absentmindedly stroked his hand and nodded throughout the duration of his speech, a single question clamoring obsessively in her brain — *"What about András?"*

She didn't dare turn on the radio in her husband's presence — this would have been tantamount to announcing her love for another man — and Raphael was still too traumatized by his ordeal to think of switching on their new TV set.

So the couple went to bed.

A sleepless night for Saffie.

The next morning, they discovered that the storm was still raging outside — thunder and icy rain at the same time — and their apartment was freezing. Another power strike! No central heating; no wireless; no coffee. Once again, the weather seemed to be in weird cahoots with political events.

Raphael had gone off to his recording studio at around ten, sullen and out of sorts. Saffie and Emil, dressed in raincoats and rubber boots, had run all the way to the Pont des Arts in the pouring rain.

That's where they are now.

But they'll go no farther, for their path is blocked by a squadron of military police. The Seine is off limits today. Emil, sensing the tension emanating from his mother and from the entire convulsed city, bursts into tears.

"But we have to go see *Apu!*" he wails, pleading with the policemen. "It's *Wednesday!*"

The uniformed men respond to his plea with German impassiveness.

"*Why* are they doing this, Mama?" asks Emil, turning to Saffie.

"I don't know yet," answers Saffie. "Let's wait a bit."

A moment later, her eyes are drawn by something on the river-bank — a purple, swollen mass that's just been hoisted out of the water by a firetruck. Saffie grabs Emil and presses his face to her stomach, as she often saw mothers do . . . back then . . . back there . . . when they wished to prevent children from seeing what they'd just seen.

"You know, Mama," says Emil as they head home, "every time the rain falls on my cheeks, it feels like I'm crying. Did that happen to you, when you were little?"

"Yes, Schatz. Yes, it did."

Funny thing about Algerians — they've got such pretty beaches in their country and they don't know how to swim; it's surprisingly easy to drown them. Even easier at night, of course, and in the middle of a violent thunderstorm. And if perchance they do know how to swim, well, you can always speed up the process with a few carefully aimed bullets.

Several dozen Algerians died this way, in Paris and the western suburbs of Paris, during the night of October 17, 1961. Drowned, with or without bullets in their heads — like András's father.

A few dozen more, including Rachid, were found in the forests on the outskirts of the capital — hanging from trees that had kept all their leaves until then, but lost them in one fell swoop that night. Strangled to death — like Saffie's mother.

Several dozen more were beaten to death in the basement of central police headquarters, right in the heart of Paris.

Of course, not all the Muslims who took part in the march that night got killed, far from it. The vast majority suffered no worse damage than the destruction of their ID cards. Eleven thousand five hundred and thirty-eight of them were merely arrested and driven out to the Palais des Sports at the Porte de Versailles. There, they were simply requested to put their hands behind their necks and move forward in an orderly fashion between two lines of policemen armed with sticks, blackjacks, heavy shoes, and rifle butts. Thanks to this, they got off with nothing but fractured skulls, smashed tibias and fibulae, broken arms and petrosal bones, bruised backs — and even those among them who were subjected to this treatment twice over didn't die, for the most part.

Finally, several hundred Algerians vanished into thin air that night. Perhaps they weren't murdered — one should always be optimistic. Perhaps they simply got tired of living in their putrid slums and decided to take off for the easy life on the beaches of Tahiti. That, too, is France.

The following Wednesday — October 25 — nearly all the Muslim corpses having been fished out of the river, the Seine is again accessible. András, however, has still not returned to his wind instruments workshop on the Rue du Roi de Sicile.

On Wednesday, November 1 — at last, at last! — he's back.

He looks ten years older. His face is hardened, marked by suffering, quivering with uncontrollable tremors. He clenches and unclenches his jaws, grinds his teeth, lights one cigarette after another. With his eyes on the floor and his voice trembling with rage, he tells Saffie about Rachid's funeral which he attended the day before. The body having been found naked and mutilated, with no ID, Rachid had been registered as an "Unknown Muslim from Algeria" and buried, along with six others like him, in communal grave n° 97 of the cemetery in Thiais. (In any case, his name had never been Rachid — all of his papers were forged.)

Of what he himself did during the twenty-four days of their separation, András speaks not a word. Not today. Not on any other day.

    .   .   .   .

"Now, now, as music always says — don't cry."

XVI

May the Lord have mercy upon us, for we are weak and fearful
— and, above all, weary.

May the Lord have mercy upon us, for we are blind and dumb
— blindfolded by our own hands, gagging on our own screams.

May the Lord have mercy upon us, for we are incapable of
healing our pain; capable only of passing it on, bequeathing it to
others as their inheritance. Here, darling.

We hop grotesquely through our time on earth, one foot in our
private lives and the other in the history of our century.

It's so difficult to be lucid. . . . And to what purpose? *Look*
(pointing), *look! This* is where you took a wrong turn; *this* is where

the first seed of evil was sown; it wasn't this man you should have met, it was . . . whom?

Ah, the dizzying arbitrariness of our choices in life. The insane entanglement of our motivations. The kaleidoscope of our misunderstandings.

Two more years go by, in public and in private.

When the Evian Agreements finally ratify the former colony's independence in March of 1962, the war has cost the lives of thirty thousand Frenchmen and over three hundred thousand Algerians.

The latter then rightfully reclaim the use and possession of all their lands and properties, including the wine-producing estate founded at the end of the nineteenth century by Monsieur Trala, Raphael Lepage's maternal grandfather.

Violent struggles break out among various military and political factions in Algeria. The country's economy is moribund, protest marches are confused and contradictory, and the FLN's provisional government sees no option but to postpone elections. A corrupt and bureaucratic dictatorship gradually takes over, fulfilling Saffie's predictions rather than those of András.

Thousands of harkis, probably as many as 150,000, are killed for having collaborated with the French. They're forced to dig their own graves, like the Jews of Berdičev. Before dying, they're forced to swallow their military decorations. Then they're castrated and dismembered; their genitalia are thrown to dogs.

Harkis aren't the only ones to be killed, however. In the city of Oran, immediately following independence, Algerians are quick to take possession of French homes, and several thousand French people are slaughtered in the melee. A massive exodus begins, as might have been predicted. Throughout the summer of 1962, pieds noirs flee the country in a panic, leaving behind all their possessions. The Jews are particularly eager to depart, having witnessed the recent adventures of their co-religionists in Tunisia and Morocco. . . . In the Marais district, the Ashkenazis who escaped deportation are rapidly submerged by waves of newly-arriving Sephardim. Yiddish and Arabic vocables jostle for elbowroom on the Rue des Rosiers, and the smell of gefilte fish vies in the air with that of falafel.

At just the same time, a certain willful and voluble minister of culture decides that something has to be done about this rundown area of Paris. The Malraux Law ordering the renovation of the Marais is passed in August of 1962, and is soon followed by a spectacular upheaval. Brothels are shut down. Shops and workshops are swept out of the courtyards of ancient mansions. Facades are sandblasted, roofs repaired, plumbing overhauled. As a result, the rats take to their heels. As a result, rats of a different kind materialize — namely, speculators. These latter order impoverished families to evacuate their apartments, cutting off their electricity and plugging their toilets to make sure they get the message. Several of András's friends are expelled from the neighborhood in this way; Madame Blumenthal, the widow on the seventh floor, manages to have her heart attack just three days before the date set for her eviction. The elderly street peddlers die, and no one comes to take their place. Motor cars rapidly evict barrows and handcarts. Coalmen and icemen are made obsolete by central heating and refrigerators. . . . The Marais grows more civilized, more bourgeois and beautiful by the day, edging its poor out toward the city limits — and before long, into the suburbs.

While most of the local trades are starting to decline and disappear, the wind instruments workshop prospers; it has, indeed, an excellent reputation, for it's in keeping with the "artistic" image that's been decided upon for the new Marais.

Of all our protagonists, it's Emil who's changed the most over the past two years.

He still has the same frail body and the same green-glinting dark eyes. But there's an anxious air about him now, and for good reason — the child is at odds with reality. Like his mother, he leads a double life; but whereas Saffie's two lives enhance and complement one another, Emil's cancel each other out. He has, is, nothing. No one has taken care to find out who he was, what he might need.

He's no longer a toddler. At the age of five and a half, he really shouldn't be here anymore. Except that he has to be here, so here he is. So. He continues to grow, casting a lengthening shadow over his mother's love. Next fall, there'll be no getting around his having to go to school. And then what? And then, no. Not then. They refuse to think about then.

When he's not with Saffie and András, Emil feels atomized, lost. He talks out loud to himself, walks around in circles in the courtyard with nothing on his mind except how to pass the time until the grown-ups reappear. He counts the quarter hours by the bells of Saint Gervais and City Hall, draws patterns with his eyes on the paving stones, exchanges small talk with neighbors or passersby. The Beatles having supplanted Ray Charles and Doris Day, he now hears *She Loves You, Yeah, Yeah, Yeah* coming from the open windows. He knows snippets and snatches of all sorts of music, but none is properly his.

He's learned to sing neither *Le Bon Roi Dagobert* nor *Alle Meine Entchen*.

He's never scuffled, quarreled, played soccer with boys of his own age.

All his acquaintances are adults — with adult know-how, adult cries and whispers, adult terrors.

He holds his breath when Raphael comes into his room to kiss him goodnight. Wipes the kiss off his forehead as soon as his father's back is turned. Studies the airplanes on the wallpaper next to his bed, imagining that Raphael is inside them — and that they crash.

"I don't like it when Papa kisses me, Mama."

"No, I know, *Schatz,* but you have to pretend. It's not so hard. Just think about something else."

Just lie, like your mother and her lover. Here, Schatz. Have another drop of poison.

In September 1963, Raphael is made a Chevalier of the Legion of Honor. He invites to the awards ceremony everyone he associates with his success — including András who, Raphael has never forgotten, expertly repaired his Rudall-Carte on the very day of his first solo concert.

In public, with no blushing or stammering, not the least outward sign of embarrassment — on the contrary, with the insolent self-confidence of people in love — Saffie and András shake hands as if they were being introduced for the first time.

We're slowly approaching the end of the story.

That same fall of 1963, Raphael goes to the United States to teach master classes on the West Coast.

When he travels like this, he doesn't really feel he is putting a distance between himself and his loved ones. The image of Saffie and Emil, his love for them, the domestic harmony in which they live, are crucial to his happiness. Raphael Lepage is an exceptional man in many ways, but from this point of view he's perfectly ordinary, banal, within the norm. Almost all family men behaved like him in 1963. What went on at home concerned them in a vague, general sort of way. Their role was to act in the outside world and to support their families financially, returning to the hearth every now and then to warm their souls, as it were. Thus, Raphael's repeated absences are by no means reprehensible or even significant — according to contemporary criteria, he's an excellent husband and father.

So it is that he finds himself in San Francisco on November 22, the day that John Fitzgerald Kennedy collapses onto the pink suit of his wife Jacqueline with blood spurting from his head. Though Raphael naturally finds the incident dramatic, he's not inordinately impressed by it. Having heard his father go on about de Tocqueville, he's always thought of the United States as a primitive, immature and violent nation.

His hosts, on the other hand, are anxious to give him a more positive image of their country, and insist on showing him the more colorful neighborhoods of San Francisco. Thus, toward the end of his stay and more or less against his will, Raphael enters a beatnik boutique, where he buys an extravagant-looking beret for Saffie — and, for Emil, a pink-and-mauve-and-purple-and-burgundy patchwork parka. The sort of article that was going to become wildly popular over the next decade — but which, when Raphael brought it back to Paris in mid-December 1963, was the only one of its kind in France.

"Thank you, Papa," Emil says gravely, trying on the multicolored coat in front of the living-room mirror and seeing that it fits him.

Beneath the voluminous hood, his face looks even more vulnerable than usual.

"How amusing!" says Saffie. She draws her purple velvet hat at a rakish angle over one eye, puts her hands on her hips and goes through a series of poses — vamp, whore, Marlene Dietrich in *A Foreign Affair*. . . .

Raphael whistles his approval, proud of his choice of gifts.

This is how things happen.

This is how people's lives unfold.

Even the weather has its part to play. Had it not been such a balmy day . . .

The first half of December had been freezing cold and wet; Emil had caught a bad cold and Saffie had remained cooped up on the Rue de Seine looking after him. This is why, on December 20, when the weather suddenly turned mild and her son's fever disappeared — and when, moreover, Raphael left early to teach his class at the Conservatory, she looked forward to the day with particular relish.

After more than five years of love, she still hungers for András's body — András's voice — András's rough hands.

"Shall we go see Edesapa?" she asks Emil. "Do you feel strong enough?"

"Oh, yes!"

She consults the thermometer on the little window balcony, the selfsame balcony over which young Raphael had leaned out to see the dead Resistance fighters. Fifteen degrees! What luck! Still, so as not to risk a relapse, she insists that Emil wear his American parka.

"But I don't *like* it! It's *pink*, it's for girls ! It makes me look *dumb!*"

"Come on, Schatz, please put it on. Just to make me happy."

In the afternoon, the temperature having risen still further, András suggests they go for a walk in the Tuileries Gardens. Emil is overjoyed — it's one of his favorite places in Paris.

The garden paths, however, are muddy and unfit for walking; all the chairs have been hooked together in long rows and carefully stacked away for the winter; a padlock blocks the entrance to the high double swings; the puppet theater is closed; so are the merry-go-round and the band pavilion. . . . The trio is starting to get discouraged — when suddenly, looking up, Emil cries out:

"*Look!*"

An unreal, a magical vision — at the far end of the garden, on the Place de la Concorde, high up and dazzling in the sunlight — a Ferris wheel.

"Can we, Mama?"

"Sure we can! Race you there!"

And so the three of them — the German woman, the Hungarian man, and the child they didn't have together — grab hands and run toward the fabulous ride. By the time they reach the ticket stand, they're panting and drenched in sweat; Emil takes off his parka and hands it to his mother.

"I'm too hot!"

When their turn in line comes, they discover to their annoyance that they only have enough money for two tickets, not three.

"Go ahead, you two," says András. "I like the firm ground. And if everyone goes up, there's no one left to watch and clap. Here, give me this. . . ."

And he takes Emil's parka from Saffie, so she won't have to hold it during the ride.

Mother and son climb into the gently rocking seat. Move slowly up into the blue sky, the pure serene sky of December. It's not frightening at all — Emil had thought he might be scared but no, everything is calm and clear and sparkling, there's no noise, no jerking — and now, describing the other arc of the circle, their seat slides slowly back down toward the ground — Mama, her green eyes luminous in the sunlight, leans forward to wave at Apu — there he is, Apu, holding my coat, smoking a cigarette and grinning as he waves at us, I just have time to see him spurt the smoke out of his nostrils all at once, like a dragon — I love it when he does that! — and we start going up again, slowly, in silence, I never dreamed Paris was so huge, it's all gray and white, gray and white as far as the eye can see, and it sparkles. . . . Saffie hugs Emil to her —

"You like it?" she asks.

"Yeah . . ."

"It makes me dizzy, but I *love* it!"

"Do you think the pigeons are wondering what we're doing up in their sky?"

Saffie laughs. The wheel comes to a halt when they're at the very top, and there's a longish wait as the lower seats change passengers.

Down on the ground, András has smoked his Gauloise to the butt, burning his fingers; he's dropped it and crushed it beneath the heel of his shoe (an old Hungarian shoe, made to measure for his father by a shoemaker friend who was later packed off to the ghetto, where he starved to death and lay rotting in the street for weeks, along with three thousand other Jewish corpses, until the Russians finally liberated the Buda sector) — now, shielding his eyes against the sun with one hand, he's trying to make out Saffie and Emil, gently rocking up there at the top of the Ferris wheel. He doesn't notice — there's no reason he should notice — the taxi that has just gone around the Place de la Concorde for the third time.

Three times is enough.

In fact once was enough, but Raphael hadn't been able to believe his eyes.

He'd asked the driver to take him straight from the Rue de Madrid to the Rue de Seine. But then, laying a hand on the front seat near the man's shoulder, he'd said,

"Excuse me . . ."

How could his voice sound so much like his normal voice, when everything inside him was cracking and splitting and collapsing?

"Yeah?"

"Would you mind going around the Place again? I thought I saw . . ."

"Yeah, sure. Long as the meter's tickin'."

Yes. It was him. André. The instrument maker.

And yes. What he had in his hand was indeed Emil's parka.

Raphael Lepage, the man who's never short of breath, who can breathe in and out at the same time, who gives breathing lessons to young flutists all over the world — has suddenly stopped breathing entirely.

"One more time," he says. The driver glances at him quizzically in the rearview mirror, then shrugs his shoulders and starts around the Place de la Concorde for the third time.

Yes. It's him.

In Raphael's head, the sunlight shatters into a million fragments.

"Now to the Rue de Seine?" the driver asks.

"Yes," says Raphael.

He's in his apartment, in their apartment, floating a few inches above the floor, his body icy, tingling, in suspension — still holding his breath, walking from room to room in this home where he thought he'd known happiness. All is clean and beautiful, and every detail of this immaculate beauty mocks and torments him — the geraniums in the window boxes, the bowl of fruit on the buffet, the blond floorboards without a particle of dust, the gleaming blue-and-white tiles in the kitchen, and the baby's room — no, Emil's room, he's not a baby anymore, but he still doesn't go to school, why has Saffie always refused to send him to school? — with the airplane-patterned wallpaper and the toys neatly lined up in rows — and their own bedroom, the bed made to perfection, the cushions smoothed and straightened, the lace curtains freshly washed and ironed, and all their clothes hanging in the closet, Raphael's to the left and Saffie's to the right, their shoes down on the floor below, brushed and polished, lined up side by side just like their owners, the man and wife who go walking through life side by side, attending concerts, dinners, the Legion of Honor ceremony. . . . "Let me introduce you to my wife . . ." "How nice to meet you!" "My wife . . ." "Madame Lepage . . ." Why hadn't she reminded him, that evening, that she and the instrument maker had already met? Why had she allowed herself to be introduced to André, András?

A savage groan rips from Raphael's throat. His entrails twist and heave. Falling to his knees next to their bed, he begins to pray, as he had the day their son was born — except that what comes to his lips this time are not the mumbled prayers he learned by rote in childhood, but rather a personal and heartfelt prayer, spewing straight from the gut — "God!" he moans. "*Please* . . . make her tell me about it when she comes home today. Make her tell me how she ran into András, how he walked them to the Ferris wheel. . . . *PLEASE, GOD, MAKE HER TELL ME!*"

Tears and snot pour from his face onto the Burgundian counterpane, meticulously stitched by his grandmother Trala during the First World War.

Saffie and Emil get home at about four-thirty, just as night is starting to fall. In the interval, Raphael has had time to pull himself together. He's splashed his face with cold water, run a comb through the remaining black curls on the back of his head, and turned on some electric lamps; now he's sitting on the couch and attempting to read *Le Monde*. But he understands not a word of what he's reading, and he's still unable to breathe.

He hears their animated voices on the landing — Emil's laughter pealing out, echoed by Saffie's. The key turns in the lock and there they are, standing right in front of him, babbling and radiant. Raphael gets to his feet and moves toward them as if in a dream; they greet him warmly — but he senses something automatic and ingenuine in their warmth.

Then, already heading for the kitchen to get dinner underway, Saffie calls out, "We went on the Ferris wheel at the Concorde!"

"Oh?" Raphael manages to say. And he sinks back down onto the couch, for his knees are too weak to carry him.

"It was fantastic!" adds Emil.

"Go run your bath now, Schatz!" calls Saffie from the kitchen.

Alone in the living room, Raphael chokes, retches, gasps for air. His life has just caved in on him, like Lotte's house the day it was bombed.

He takes his evening meal in a daze, looking back and forth from one to the other — if they lie so convincingly, so nonchalantly, lying must be a habit for them.

"A little more gratin Dauphinois?"

"No, thank you."

"Aren't you hungry? I hope you haven't caught Emil's cold."

"No, I'm fine."

Emil's cold. A little more gratin. He must be dreaming. He didn't really see what he saw.

. . . .

It's his turn to spend a sleepless night, next to his peacefully slumbering wife. Saffie breathes deeply and regularly, exhaling a faint sigh of contentment every now and then. Is she dreaming about. . . ? How long? . . . Never, thinks Raphael, more agitated by the minute, has she cried out the other man's name during lovemaking. But then . . . never has she cried out my name, either.

At four o'clock in the morning, unable to bear it any longer, he gets up and starts pacing back and forth in the living room.

At six o'clock, he comes to a decision: he must find some way of getting Emil alone and questioning him. But how? Emil never leaves Saffie's side. At the age of six, he's still tangled up in her apron strings. That's bad, Raphael suddenly realizes. It's unhealthy. It's monstrous.

At seven — Hortense Trala-Lepage has always been an early riser — he dials the number of the house in Burgundy.

At eight, when Saffie finally emerges from their bedroom, tying the belt of the gold-embroidered black kimono he gave her for her twenty-fifth birthday, he announces,

"I'm taking Emil to Burgundy this afternoon."

"What?" she says, blinking, her voice still thick with sleep.

He pours her a cup of coffee.

"My mother called," he says (if you can tell lies, so can I). "She begged me to bring him down to see her. . . . Mama's not getting any younger, you know. . . . And since the shock of Algeria, her health isn't what it used to be. . . . Emil's her only heir. . . . Please, Saffie — try to put yourself in her place. Try to forgive her."

"How long will you be gone?"

"We can be there and back in twenty-four hours. She just wants to meet him, give him his Christmas present. . . . Emil's nearly six years old and he's never met his only living grandparent — it's unnatural!"

Saffie doesn't contradict him. She keeps her head down, her eyes glued to the bottom of her coffee cup. Then, raising the cup to her lips, she takes a sip of coffee — to hide (or so it seems to Raphael) the suggestion of a smile.

"Yes, all right," she says. "I can understand your mother."

"Do you think you can survive for a whole day without your son?" he asks, with a touch of perversity.

"I'll survive."

He hates her.

XVII

So here are Raphael and Emil, at one o'clock in the afternoon, sitting silently in the taxi that is taking them to Gare de Lyon. It's the first time the two of them have gone anywhere alone together.

And here, at the same instant, is Saffie running joyously in the rain — it's the first time she has gone to see her lover alone. She won't be spending the night at his place (she knows the concierge keeps track of her comings and goings), but she'll stay for dinner, lounge around in bed . . . On the Pont des Arts, a gust of wind turns her umbrella inside out and she laughs out loud for joy.

Silence reigns between Emil and Raphael, alone together in their train compartment. Outside, the landscape is dismal and monotonous, and rain whips relentlessly at the train window. Steam has formed on the pane, and Emil is tracing patterns on it with his fingers. He studies the movements of the raindrops on the glass, just as on the long-ago day of *Qué sera, sera* in András's workshop (of which he has no memory) — but this time their paths are violently inflected by the speed of the train.

Raphael is restless and agitated. He doesn't know how to frame the questions he wants to ask his son.

András opens the door for his mistress, whose cheeks are red from the cold. He takes the umbrella from her, shakes it open, and props it up in a corner. ("It is *masculine*, umbrella? No, I don't believe it! A so-feminine object! For me it's feminine!") Turning around, he holds his arms out to Saffie and she rushes into them.

"I can stay late!" she murmurs. "Emil went to Burgundy with Raphael."

In the Paris-Lyons-Marseille train, the cross-examination has begun. Emil doesn't jump when his father pronounces András's name, but he blinks several times. Raphael sees this, and it's all the confession he needs — the child's ensuing denials are useless. He corners his son, hounds him, bombards him with questions. Emil is panic-stricken. Who is this man? He doesn't know him, he's never seen him before. He begins to whimper in fear. Beside himself, Raphael delivers two terrible blows, one to each of Emil's ears, that leave the child's head ringing.

Father and son sit there staring at each other. Until today they'd never looked at one another very closely. This goes on for two or three seconds, and then Raphael collapses. Sobs in front of Emil, crushes him to his chest, implores his forgiveness. The boy is even more terrified by his father's weakness than by his strength. Extricating himself from the jiggly wet embrace, he utters an irrevocable condemnation.

"Leave me alone. . . . You never paid any attention to us anyway. *He's* my real father."

Raphael's whole body arches up in pain.

Saffie's body arches up in pleasure. She's weeping, like the very first time they made love, clasping András's muscled back between her crossed legs. For once she doesn't need to stifle her cries for Emil's sake — she can let herself go if she likes. And she does. Let herself. Go. Very far.

Raphael: a disarticulated puppet sprawled on the seat of the train. Again, silence has fallen between him and his son. He recalls Saffie's godawful silence during her pregnancy. . . . How she has changed since then! And what a fool he was to believe that it was thanks to marriage and motherhood. . . .

The hours slide by, flat and gray and uneventful. Rocked by the regular noise and movement of the train, Raphael manages to fall asleep, momentarily freeing himself from the hell of consciousness.

Emil's arm on his shoulder wakes him with a start — and the nightmare comes to reclaim him.

"I'm hungry," murmurs Emil. "It's five o'clock and I haven't had any snack."

Raphael slaps himself into wakefulness. Grabs his head with both hands and rubs his balding pate furiously.

"You're right," he mutters. "I didn't think to bring you a snack. Let's go to the dining car, they must have hot chocolate or something."

András brings a cup of rum-laced tea to Saffie, who's still stretched out in bed. He lights a Gauloise and studies his mistress through the spirals of smoke, admiring the precise and natural movements of her naked body.

"I love you, Saffie."

She looks up, meets his eyes.

"I love you, András."

Emil goes first, and Raphael leans over his shoulder to open the heavy sliding doors. In the vestibules between cars, he takes his son's hand to help him across the metallic platform, whose overlapping metal plates jerk and slide unpredictably beneath their feet. He can see that Emil is frightened by the tumult of noise and wind — and remembers how frightened he used to be, as a child, in this same situation. Lurching and staggering, they move through the train — six, seven, eight cars — passing from stifling heat to icy cold, from calm to uproar. The effort of opening and closing the heavy doors leaves Raphael a little more weary each time. His sleepless night has exhausted him, his brief nap did nothing but muddy his thoughts — and now, lighting up like a torch in his brain, the question he'd meant to ask Emil comes back to him — *when did it start?*

"How long has this thing been going on?" he asks in a low voice, as they go lurching down the corridor of the ninth car.

But Emil, traumatized by the blows to his ears, has resolved not to say another word. If only Mama were here to help him!

Raphael suddenly realizes they must be heading in the wrong direction. They were probably not far from the dining car when they set out, and now they'll have to retrace their steps — all the way back and farther still — opening and closing doors, holding hands in the vestibules. . . . It seems beyond his strength. Not wanting to admit to his son that they're going the wrong way, he keeps advancing doggedly toward the rear of the train, all the while repeating his question insistently, louder and louder:

"How long has it been going on? When did you meet András for the first time?"

As in a nightmare, the train's resistance and Emil's seem to be one and the same thing; Raphael senses that no matter what he does, the dining car and the answer to his question will elude him forever. . . . Now they've reached the last car — a baggage compartment. One of its doors has been left wide open onto the tracks. His nerves at breaking point, overwhelmed by a generalized sense of failure, Raphael wheels around to confront Emil:

"You have to tell me!"

He needs to scream to make himself heard above the noise whipping in through the open door, and this outward sign of rage provokes real rage in him. Wedging his feet in the doorway, he grabs the boy under the armpits and thrusts him out above the rushing ground.

"Papa! Papa!"

"Yes, PAPA!" screams Raphael. *"Yes, I'm your papa, and don't you ever forget it!"*

His rage intensifies still further, exacerbated by the earsplitting racket of the train as it goes hurtling down the tracks at top speed, its shrieking and rattling tons of metal reflecting the hubbub in his brain —

"Who did you say your papa was? Me or him?"

"You! You!" screams Emil in panic.

"And how long has this thing been going on?" screams Raphael, shaking him like a rag doll.

But Emil, made breathless by fear and by the mad buffeting of the wind, is unable to answer. His legs pedal wildly in the air as he tries to get a foothold on the doorledge.

And the next instant, he's gone.

András has put on a new record — Roland Kirk, the phenomenal blind musician, playing strichophone and nasal flute at the same time. While Saffie gets dressed, he goes out to the Rue des Ecouffes and buys them some Tunisian pastries — gazelle horns, zlabias, sashbakias, and makrouds. . . . He finds them less heavy than the Apfelstrudel and Mohnkuchen from Central Europe.

It's the first time the two of them have had "dinner" together. Afterward, sticky with honey and giggling like kids, they suck each other's fingers. Make love all over again, almost without undressing, amid the dust and cigarette butts on the floor — Saffie's head banging against chair legs, every assault of András's body making her convulse and moan.

Raphael pulls on the lever of the alarm signal to stop the train.

Saffie smooths her hair in front of the little mirror over the sink. She puts on her boots and coat, slips her umbrella under her arm and walks across the courtyard, pressing András's large body to her side. In the middle of the street they kiss one last time, allowing the cool rain to mingle with the warmth of their saliva. And then — it's only eight-thirty — she leaves him. Opens her umbrella and advances wide-eyed through the city. Walks past the Samaritaine department store, magnificently decorated for Christmas. Heads toward the Seine, marveling to find herself alone and strong in the most beautiful city in the world.

It's already happened, and she doesn't know it. Emil is already dead, his skull split open instantly the moment he hit the rocky ground — this is a fact — but the fact hasn't yet found its way into his mother's head, which is still pulsating with love and music.

Does it really have to find its way there? For the time being, it's a fact known to so few people that it has virtually no meaning. Apart from Raphael, the only ones who know about it are the conductor, two ticket inspectors, and a handful of passengers annoyed by the train's untimely halt. Couldn't we just leave things as they are? Couldn't time stop here, and the story come to an end? Are we really obliged to go on with it, to describe how this fact engendered others, and then still others — always facts, facts, nothing but facts?

The police have been informed. Already, the telephone is ringing in the third-floor apartment on the Rue de Seine. But no one's there to answer it. Alone on the Pont des Arts, Saffie is dancing in the rain.

.   .   .   .   .   .

Hortense Trala-Lepage finally manages to reach the concierge, startling her out of a deep sleep at nine o'clock (she goes to bed early now, knocked out by the combined effects of her evening pastis and the analgesic she takes for her phlebitis).

And so it is that Lisette Blanche, in a terrycloth robe and in tears, settles into an armchair next to the window to watch for Madame Lepage.

She feels no jubilation whatsoever, believe me. She's a woman of extraordinary kindness.

.   .   .   .   .   .

"An accident." For the duration of his trial, which lasts for the better part of 1964, the world-famous flutist Raphael Lepage sticks obstinately to his version of the story. "He slipped — the wind tore him from my hands — I did everything in my power to save him. . . ."

As there were no witnesses, he'll be acquitted. But we were there, and we know the truth. We know the enormity of the despair that made him loosen his grip on his son's rib cage for just a fraction of a second.

.   .   .   .   .   .

As for Saffie, she disappeared. No one in Paris ever saw her again. The morning after Emil's death, when the police arrived on the Rue de Seine and rang the third-floor doorbell, there remained not the slightest trace of Saffie's passage through Raphael's existence.

She'd simply vanished into thin air. And the concierge, for once, hadn't seen a thing.

Even I have no idea what became of my heroine. We know so little of one another. . . . It's so easy to lose touch. Of course, we can always speculate — she had a French passport; perhaps she decided to carve out a new life for herself in Spain . . . or Canada. . . . But if this is so, it took place outside of our story. The truth of our story is that she disappeared.

As we shall all disappear, in the end.

EPILOGUE

With a single word, let's jump forward another thirty-five years. . . . Ah! here we are at the end of the twentieth century.

Almost all French people now own television sets, telephones, and private toilets; a large proportion of them even own personal computers. Germany and France are best friends — they're building Europe together, and dream of having a common army someday. The Berlin Wall has come tumbling down, provoking the demise of all the communist regimes in Central Europe in rapid succession. Hungary is the country that most gracefully managed the transition from a controlled to a market economy (no one says "capitalist" anymore). As for Algeria, thirty years of socialist corruption and bureaucracy have revived old dreams of religious rigor; the country is in the throes of a bloody and interminable civil war.

Paris is Paris, more insolently gorgeous and in love with luxury than ever. You no longer have to pay to sit in park chairs, but if you want a glass of water on a café terrace it'll cost you an arm and a leg. Street urinals have been replaced by fancy pay toilets, complete with automatic flush and classical music. Charles de Gaulle is nothing but the name of an airport and a metro station, but Parisians prefer to say Roissy and Etoile, sowing confusion in the minds of tourists. Although the slums have been torn down, hideous working-class suburbs are filled to overflowing with the French-born children and grandchildren of Algerians, incensed at their lack of prospects for the future, or even for the present. Brigitte Bardot castigates them for the annual ritual murder of thousands of innocent lambs. Unemployment is endemic and apparently unstoppable. On the Rue des Rosiers, the employees of Goldenberg's delicatessen will readily show you the machine-gun bullet marks left by a terrorist attack in August of 1982. Fifty yards down the street, the old hammam has been revamped and transformed, first into a Western clothes shop, then a kosher pizzeria, and finally a fancy tea room. The Marais as a whole has become one of the nerve centers of Paris fashion.

Our story ends where it began — namely, at the Gare du Nord, where Saffie set foot on French soil for the first time. Or, to be precise, directly across from the train station, at the Terminus Nord brasserie.

It's a chilly, gloomy, rainy day — like an inordinate number of days in Paris, if truth be told. It could be March or November; there's no way of knowing.

It's two o'clock in the afternoon and Raphael Lepage, who's just gotten back from reunified Berlin on a high-speed train, is eating sauerkraut with meat and washing it down with an excellent Riesling. He's acquired a taste for German cooking in recent years.

Using the linen napkin with the initials TN embroidered on it, he wipes goose grease from his thin flutist's lips. He's in very good shape for his age — sixty-nine. He still has a certain style about him. Of course, he's portlier than he used to be — and all he has left in the way of hair is a narrow tonsure of white curls — but if you look at his face closely enough, it's perfectly recognizable. Yes, the same nose, the same cheekbones — and, behind his spectacles, the same warm brown eyes.

Setting aside the newspaper he was reading as he ate, he glances up . . . and freezes. On a stool at the counter, just a few yards away from him — is it possible? — reflected in the wall of mirrors, so that Raphael sees him simultaneously from the front and from the back — yes, there's no doubt about it — András. Smoking a cigarette and drinking coffee with calvados. Unbelievably aged. His longish hair, now entirely gray, is gathered in a ratty ponytail. A chaotic network of lines makes his face resemble a field ploughed by a madman. He's wearing rimless glasses and a red scarf — ah yes, some diehards have never given up their dreams of revolution. . . .

Setting his linen napkin down on the table, Raphael gets to his feet. Moves slowly forward. Crosses the restaurant without taking his eyes off the mirror. Now his own reflection appears in it, grows gradually larger, then comes to a stop next to András's — at which point, András looks up.

The two men's gazes meet in the mirror.

They're elderly, you understand. In their old men's disguise — white hair, wrinkles, glasses — they now look a great deal alike. You must have noticed this — how elderly people seem to recover an air of innocence. Merciful time comes to rub an eraser across their minds and bodies, blurring their distinctive traits, wiping out their memories — dissolving, one by one, the harsh lessons life has inflicted on them. . . . One forgets, you know. . . . Oh yes, one forgets. . . .

Nothing happened, did it? Or . . . so little . . . and such a long time ago. . . . Tantamount to nothing by now . . . isn't it? Wouldn't that be preferable?

We must, after all, recover our innocence before going to meet the angel.

Ah yes. All of us are innocent still.

András and Raphael stare at each other in the mirror. András neither flinches nor turns on his stool to confront Raphael in the flesh; they exchange neither a word nor a handshake. What's going on between the two of them as they share this endless silent gaze? A long time ago, each deprived the other of the woman and child he loved. And now, both are testing their hearts — is the pain still there? Can the flames of hatred still be revived, or have the last embers finally died out?

They continue to stare at each other. Sincerely, almost serenely. We don't see them separate.

And that's the end?

Oh, no. I promise you it's not.

All you have to do is look up — it's going on around you all the time.

NANCY HUSTON was born in Calgary, Alberta in 1953 and moved to New Hampshire when she was fifteen. As a student at Sarah Lawrence College, she went to Paris in 1973 for a year of study abroad and never moved back. She is the author of seven novels and numerous works of nonfiction that have been published in her native Canada and her adopted France, and she writes in both French and English. Her previous books have won the Prix Goncourt des Lycéens, the Prix du Livre Inter, the Prix Elle (Québec), and the Governor General's Award for Fiction in French. Her books have also been shortlisted for the Prix Goncourt (twice), the Prix Fémina (twice) and the Governor General's Award for Fiction in English. *The Mark of the Angel,* a bestseller in France, and winner of the Grand Prix des Lectrices de Elle, is Huston's U.S. debut. She lives in Paris with her husband, Tzvetan Todorov, a philosopher and writer originally from Bulgaria, and their two children.

A NOTE ON THE BOOK

THE TEXT for this book was composed by Steerforth
Press using a digital version of Granjon, a typeface designed by George W. Jones and first issued by Linotype in
1928. This book was printed on acid free papers and bound
with traditional smythe sewing by BookPress~Quebecor of
Brattleboro, Vermont.